The War of the Sexes

The War of the Sexes

by
Odette Dulac

translated, annotated and introduced by
Brian Stableford

A Black Coat Press Book

ISBN 978-1-61227-405-8. First Printing. May 2015. Published by Black Coat Press, an imprint of Hollywood Comics.com, LLC, P.O. Box 17270, Encino, CA 91416. All rights reserved. Except for review purposes, no part of this book may be reproduced or transmitted in any form or by any means, electronic or mechanical, including photocopying, recording, or by any information storage and retrieval system, without permission in writing from the publisher. The stories and characters depicted in this novel are entirely fictional. Printed in the United States of America.

Introduction

The book usually listed in bibliographies as ...*tel qu'il est!* [As it Is] by Odette Dulac, here translated as *The War of the Sexes*, was first published by J. Snell et Cie. in 1926. The front cover and title page of the Snell edition preface the ellipsis at the beginning of the title with a drawing of the figure usually known in English as a Cupid, but more commonly known in French as an *Amour*, so the title should be construed as "[*Amour*] *tel qu'il est*"— which could be translated it into English as *[Sex] As it Is*. The original title is a modification of part of the title of the first of Voltaire's *contes philosophiques*, "Le Monde comme il va" [The World as it Goes] (1748; usually translated as "Babouk"), embodying the phrase that came to serve as a manifesto for the whole set, and the whole subgenre: to use fantastic materials satirically in order to show the world "as it is," and not as it is represented or believed to be by contemporary error and hypocrisy. Variations of the phrase were used by numerous other French satirists, so it was easily recognizable by French readers; the same is not true, however, of its English equivalent, so I thought it better to substitute something that communicates a simpler idea of the novel's subject-matter. It is as well to bear in mind, however, that its real theme, however paradoxical its method might be, is [*Amour*] *as it is*.

"Odette Dulac" was the stage-name adopted by Jeanne Latrilhe (1865-1939) when she made her debut as an actress and singer in 1892, at an unusually late age for debutants on the Parisian stage. The autobiography that she wrote late in life leaves a seven-year gap prior to her arrival in Paris, about which nothing is said, during which time the seeds were presumably sown of her subsequent metamorphoses. She first made a name for herself performing in comic operas, but became even more famous when she launched a parallel career in the cabarets of Montmartre as a singer and performer in satirical sketches and revues in 1897, which eventually took over all her activity. She became one of the most popular *artistes* in Paris during the first few years of the 20th century, and also made a brief but successful appearance in London, famously singing "The Honeysuckle and the Bee," but she quit the stage abruptly in 1904 after a quarrel with her director. She then launched an entirely new career as a sculptor, primarily in wax, and as a writer active in the cause of women's rights.

Her first novel, *Le Droit au plaisir* [The Right to Pleasure] (1908), is an epistolary text in the tradition of Jean-Jacques Rousseau's *Julie, ou la nouvelle Héloïse* (1761; tr. as *The New Heloise*), in which a marquise dissatisfied with her sex life obtains hypothetical explanations and practical suggestions from an artiste, who attempts to use analogies drawn from Jean-Henri Fabre's *Souvenirs entomologiques* (10 volumes, 1879-1909; best-known in English via the sampler *Fabre's Book of Insects*, 1921) to cast light on the differences between male and female desire. If that argumentative strategy seems a trifle odd now, it is worth noting that it was by no means out of keeping with the spirit of the times, appearing five years after Remy de Gourmont's classic study of *Physique de l'Amour* (1903; tr. as *The Natural Philosophy of Love*), which similarly makes use of insect analogies in order to cast light on the quirks of human sexuality, continuing a rich tradition of comparisons and quirky identifications that extended from Fabre and the scientific popularizations of S. Henry Berthoud through Maurice Maeterlinck's

La Vie des abeilles (1901; tr. as *The Life of the Bee*) and Han Ryner's *L'Homme-fourmi* (1901)[1]. Significantly, however, Dulac employs her own analogies, which have implications more sinister and savage than those preferred even by conscientiously decadent Romantics.

In Dulac's second novel, *Le Silence des femmes* [The Silence of Women] (1910), her feminist opinions became more strident and more direct, as she launched a scathing attack on social and religious hypocrisy regarding contemporary sexual mores, and the terrible effects such hypocrisies frequently had on the lives of young women. The outbreak of the Great War, which caused a massive disruption of those mores, the results of which horrified many observers, called forth an even stronger reaction from Dulac in *La Houille rouge, les enfants de la violence* [Red Coal (or, in a more general sense, energy): The Children of Violence] (1916), which added to the accentuation of the problems pointed out in the earlier novel the particular problems of young women who gave birth to children as a result of rape by the invading Germans and cajolery on the part of young men departing for the Front. *Faut-Il?* [Is it Necessary?] (1919) reflected on the legacy of the war in a more sober and sentimental vein.

Dulac's journalistic work became more varied after the end of the Great War, but her novels continued insistently to tackle controversial themes associated with sexuality: syphilis in *L'Enfer d'une étreinte* [The Inferno of an Embrace] (1922) and homosexuality in *Les Désexués* [The Desexualized] (1926, in collaboration with Charles Étienne). *[Amour]...tel qu'il est!* does not break this pattern, and is, in a sense, a kind of philosophical summary of

---

[1] tr. as *The Human Ant*, Black Coat Press, ISBN 978-1-61227-323-5.

the themes of the author's first three novels, but it takes a gigantic leap sideways in terms of its narrative method, and perhaps an equally giant step forward in modeling the problems identified therein. It would be overstating the case to say that it suggests a solution to the problems, although the narrative does adopt a proudly prophetic, not to say apocalyptic, tone, but it certainly attempts to encapsulate the entire issue, and to pay homage to its awkwardness in the sheer bizarrerie that it considers to be required in order to accomplish that encapsulation.

The insectile analogies introduced in *Le Droit au plaisir* are greatly elaborated in *[Amour]...tel qu'il est!* to produce an extremely strange fanciful account of sexual biology, which is carefully based in an improvised astrological theory of evolution. All of that is further parceled in an idiosyncratic mysticism based in Buddhist and Hindu ideas, as doubly filtered through the reinterpretations of the theosophist feminist Annie Besant and—more particularly—the "anthroposophist" Rudolf Steiner, with many further embellishments that are the author's own. The result of that triple layering of fantastic notions, much of which is made explicit but which nevertheless retains a rich halo of hints and oblique implications, is a unique literary construct that had no parallel at the time the novel was written, and still seems highly unusual today, when adventurous hybridizations of speculative fiction and quasi-religious fantasy are considerably more familiar.

In fact, *[Amour]...tel qu'il est* is so bizarre that it seems that hardly anyone knew, at the time of its publication, what to make of it, and people still have difficulty. In the French version of Odette Dulac's Wikipedia entry, which is otherwise very extensive, only the title is presently mentioned, with no commentary. In the shorter English version, the title is mangled and attributed to the wrong story-line. The only person, so far as I can detect, who has ever called attention to the book in a moderately complimentary fashion is Pierre Versins, in his *Encyclopédie de l'utopie, des voyages extraordinaires et de la science-fiction* (1972), who describes it as "rather remarkable" and lists a few of the exotic ideas featured in it, taking them out of context in order to emphasize their boldness, but does not attempt any further analysis of the text.

Many commentators might have been put off the idea of attempting any such analysis by simply not knowing where to start. Although the Voltairean title clearly suggests that the narrative is satirical, it is related in a seemingly heartfelt tone of deadly earnest, which gives no obvious hint of any sarcastic or satirical intent. That kind of deliberate self-contradiction is familiar is the context of orally-narrated tall stories, in which the most ludicrous absurdities are presented with a perfectly straight face, deliberately confusing the hearer, but that is a kind of practical joke, and *[Amour]...tel qu'il est!* is certainly not a joke; it does not present its strange ideas with the intention of trying to trick readers into taking them seriously before subjecting them to ridicule. It should be remembered, however, that the whole point of Voltairean *contes philosophiques* is, indeed, philosophical, and that they sometimes present worlds-within-texts that are frankly absurd in order to give readers an Archimedean lever long enough, and a place to stand, from which it might be possible to move their perception of the real world.

The question of the extent to which Odette Dulac might actually have believed any of the mystical or biological ideas suggested in *[Amour]...tel qu'il est!* is simply not relevant to the kind of story it is and the kind of effect at which it is aiming. On one level, the novel's inventions are mind-bogglingly absurd—but the point of that

9

absurdity is to invite the reader to consider whether the absurd explanation might make more sense of the puzzling phenomena that it addresses than any conventional explanation that could possibly be offered.

In that sense, the nested sets of exotic hypotheses that the novel puts forward—mystical, evolutionary and physiological—are, without a doubt, an imaginative *tour de force*. There is nothing stranger in the entirety of imaginative literature (which is a compliment in itself) and yet, the account thus offered of the underlying logic (or illogic) war of the sexes suggests a coherency missing from many then-conventional hypotheses endeavoring to explain the puzzling features of human sexuality. It foreshadows, in more ways than one, such clownishly serious endeavors as John Gray's best-selling *Men are from Mars, Women are from Venus* (1992), whose author trained for some years, before establishing himself as a bona fide relationship counselor, with the Maharishi Mahesh Yogi.

There is no doubt that *[Amour]...tel qu'il est!* is a rather challenging book in terms of the requests it makes of the readers "willing suspension of disbelief," but the rewards it offer are commensurately considerable. It must have been a difficult book to write, too, and not only because it required imaginative contortions and gymnastics never attempted before. Indeed, the book carries a dedication to "Madame Sylvie Valmath...firstly because she possesses a charming heart and a highly evolved soul, but also because she alone knows the act of courage and faith that this book represents."

As well as courage and faith, the writing of the novel must have required the hope that it would not be met by a solid wall of scorn or indifference—a hope that was probably only vindicated to a slight degree in 1926, but which was nevertheless not entirely forlorn. Nowadays, when the kinds of imaginative materials that the text deploys are more familiar, and there is a much larger population of readers potentially able and willing to appreciate the boldness and ingenuity of their particular combination, it is probably in a better position to be appreciated.

It would be inappropriate to go into more detail here about the details of the imaginative schema set out in the plot, because it would function as a spoiler, but I shall add an afterword to the text addressing a few of the most intriguing questions that the author leaves (deliberately, one presumes) conspicuously unanswered.

This translation was made from a copy of the 1926 Snell edition. The layout of the text in the original version is as innovative as the text itself; there are no numbered chapters, although the three lessons of Brahma are titled and preceded by page-breaks. All the other text breaks are indicated by lines of dots, which are sometimes single, sometimes double, sometimes triple and in one case quadruple, although the number of lines of dots does not correspond proportionately with the lapses of time between scenes. I have retained the breaks in question exactly as they appear in the original, taking the view that they are a significant, albeit enigmatic, feature of the text.

Brian Stableford

THE WAR OF THE SEXES
[AMOUR]...AS IT IS

"Oh, the Crazy Rock! The rock..."

"Where?"

"There...it was there five minutes ago—and now it's disappeared!"

"Hallucination."

"No, no—I too saw, just now on that rock, another rock forming a vague triangle. That's it's no longer there is perfectly true."

"Oh, the power of legend! You believe in it, then, this vagabond rock that appears and disappears in people's faces, in any corner of the forest of Fontainebleau?"

"Oh, pardon me—only within a three-kilometer radius of Barbizon."[2]

"It must be a phantom of a painter of the Millet school. He doubtless had a heart of stone, and is manifest in the form that best expresses his remorse."

This rather strange dialogue took place on the fourteenth of December 1913, on the threshold of one of the grottoes made of tangled sandstone blocks that abound along the footpaths of Cuvier-Chatillon. Three hunters were lurking there in order to try to surprise a superb wild

---

[2] Odette Dulac spent the latter years of her life living, writing and sculpting in Barbizon, where there is now a street named after her. The town's most famous former inhabitant was the landscape painter Jean-François Millet (1814-1875) who founded a "Barbizon school" of painting with Théodore Rousseau (1812-1867), to which numerous direct and indirect references are made in the novel.

boar they had been tracking since the morning. The barking of the hounds indicated that they might hope to have it within range of their rifles soon.

No sounds of flight, however, troubled the silence of their expectation. Only a little dry cough broke the sensuality of their ambush, and a curse expressed their disappointment on seeing a respectable old lady advancing at a slow pace. She was very simply dressed, but her entire attitude was so mystical, grave and noble that they bowed as she passed by.

She sketched the vague salute with which a woman of the world acknowledges the courtesy of a man who steps aside, and then she drew away, not without letting her gaze weigh upon the youngest of the hunters. The latter immediately thought that his heart was about to fail. The lady disappeared unhurriedly behind a rock, and it was only after an interval of a few minutes that he was able to murmur:

"Upon my word, if that woman's eyes were shining in a younger face, you could get your black suits ready, Messieurs, because I wouldn't be long delayed in marrying her. Sapristi! What softness! What a gleam! I still can't get over it!"

"She'd do a lot better to stay by her fireside," said the most heavily-bearded of the three Nimrods.

"Shh! Listen to the dogs. The beast's coming toward us again... Flay was leading just now...I can't hear his voice any longer...yes...a cry. The animal has thrown off the dog...look out...look out..."

An indescribable racket was indeed approaching, when a rifle-shot cut it short. A momentary silence followed, and then the barking redoubled in intensity.

Suddenly, a horrible brown mass, stinking, growling and low on its legs emerged between two tall rocks and raced along the path. Three gunshots immediately put it down, and its cadaver completely blocked the narrow corridor in which the drama had unfolded. The dogs, the beaters and a dozen hunters soon found a means of getting round it, however, and there was a long palaver before it was decided to carry it away. That was scarcely easy in that tortuous terrain, but the classic cortege ended up forming. Behind the porters of the victim, the victors followed in single file, all their pipes lit.

Before quitting the grotto, where he had remained somewhat apart, the one enamored of the old lady scanned the surroundings with his gaze…and stood there open-mouthed. There, ten meters away, the rock loomed up again.

Incapable of overcoming the irrational terror that invaded him, he started running forward, jumping over all the obstacles that he could, and colliding with his hunting companions.

"Have you got the devil on your heels?" one of them asked.

"Yes," he replied, gravely. "The rock—the Crazy Rock—appeared in front of me."

"Where? Where? Show us!"

"Don't laugh! Obviously, I must be suffering…a hallucination, undoubtedly. But I swear to you that I saw it rise up and set itself in equilibrium on rock B."

"The one that serves to attract the rock-climbers of the Alpine Club?"

"That I don't know."

A polite silence descended upon the group of hunters, whose mocking eyes looked the visionary up and down.

"Is the fellow a little touched?" asked Robert Dunant, who passed for the strong mind of the band, in a low voice.

"No, Monsieur," replied one of the gamekeepers. "Or if he is, there are plenty like him. In the last six months we've almost all seen the phenomenon."

"How is it manifest?"

Very simply. One is walking along, looking at everything and nothing. Without looking for it, one sees a gray mass, heavy and mossy, posed on top of larger block. That's not surprising, is it? There are plenty of little rocks on top of big rocks in the forest. But when, suddenly, you no longer sees the solid triangle where it was a moment before, well, it gives you quite a shock; you get goosepimples and turn round. I'm a gamekeeper, I'm not afraid of wild boar, nor poachers, but I don't like to encounter the Crazy Rock. Madame Wiscorney can laugh at me, and try all the time to catch a glimpse of the thing in question, but personally, I'd rather not."

"Who's this Madame Wiscorney?"

"An old lady, very good, very worthy and very tranquil, who loves the forest even more than her house. She's been living here for a long time with her granddaughter— a pretty girl of sixteen."

"Quite bizarre!" the questioner murmured, striking a light. "That's an enigma I'd like to solve."

....
....
....

Three hours later, all the hunters were finishing dinner at the Hôtel des Charmettes, in a room whose windows overlooked the main street. As befits those sorts of celebratory feasts, the menu had been succulent, washed down with generous wines and seasoned with spicy stories. Among those at table, admitted for the first time to the honor of hunting with his father, was young Montala. He was an adolescent of twenty-two, whose face had the beauty of a Roman mask and his body the suppleness and vigor of modern sportsmen.

There was also—at the third invitation—Louis Dubar, a young advocate still in training, and a very amiable guest. The latter had paid his entry fee in savory anecdotes, and he had just started a new one when he interrupted himself to say: "But...there she is! It's her! Oh, that woman's eyes!"

All the men looked into the street then, where the old lady they had encountered that morning at Cuvier-Chatillon was passing by on the opposite sidewalk. She was escorted by two adorable young women, equal in charm but different in type, one brunette and one blonde. Each of their elegant silhouettes had the finest of profiles.

No one saw Pierre Montala blush, for his father immediately said: "Ah! You noticed the Hindu woman's eyes! Admirable, aren't they? Those are her granddaughters accompanying her. They're rarely together nowadays, even though they were born twins. Their mother died giving birth to them, and the two grandmothers, paternal and maternal, one Catholic and the other Buddhist, made a kind of theosophical contest out of the education of the two children. Each one wanted to prove the excellence of her religion for modeling the soul. Madame Wiscorney is a very curious individual, and is reputed to be one of the greatest Asiatic Initiates."

"Much better to be a cordon bleu!" quipped Robert Dunant.

"Perhaps. All I know is that the two sisters only come together for a week or ten days every year. Their meetings give rise to joyful family scenes. Madame Wiscorney, sure of the heart and mind of Maya, gives her complete freedom to confide her impressions to her sister Ghislaine, but Madame d'Angeville, an intransigent devotee, is fearful on behalf of her little brunette of heretical theories, which might give rise to doubt. 'Doubt! Demolisher of Temples and poisoner of wellbeing!' as she delights in repeating, signing herself three times."

"I assume that the young women talk to one another about other things than the Gospel and the Bhagavad-Gita?" said the incorrigible Robert Dunant.

"Undoubtedly, undoubtedly! But the two old ladies, both intelligent, know full well that amour won't take long to mount an assault on their wards' hearts. It's then that one or other will triumph, and each of them is preparing her victory, one by taking her granddaughter to sermons and the other by taking hers into the forest. One believes in the demon, the other in the daimon..."

"Yes, but it's still a question of a man!"

"Naturally! Whether one puts horns or goat's feet on him, whether he reeks of sulfur or sweat, it's always the poor male that turns the heads of virgins. 'The work of the flesh,' as Madame d'Angeville says, or 'the Sacred Feast,' as Madame Wiscorney calls it, is the most redoubtable adventure in the life of a woman!"

"I've never doubted it!" said the merry guests, in chorus. "A little glass in honor of the great uncomprehended!"

"Waiter! A fine vintage, for a toast to amour!"

Coarse laughter blended, and in a deafening racket, there was talk of "chicks" who... and of Lampitos[3] who... In brief, the ordinary good cheer of hunters after drinking gave Virtue a beating, with abridged memories.

---

[3] Lampito is the Spartan woman who assists Lysistrata to arrange a sex strike in Aristophanes' comedy.

Only Pierre Montala kept silent. Suddenly, as if Gallic chatter might shock a chaste ear—he cried imperiously: "Shh! Shut up! They're coming back."

The two grandmothers and the two young women about whom they had been talking were, indeed, going along the street. Maya was laughing while walking backwards. The dimples in her slightly-suntanned cheeks, compared with the brightness of her teeth, gave the impression of nests were little birds were dreaming. Beneath the gilded shadow of long lashes, her eyes, more green than blue, allowed an amiable gaze to fall on things, but so luminous that it seemed to make everything on which its settled sparkle. There was within them a little of the strange radiation that rendered Madame Wiscorney's eyes so attractive and unforgettable.

Next to her, eyelids lowered, Ghislaine was walking serenely. The expression of confused and enraptured joy with which Raphael bathed the face of the Virgin listening to the Angel Gabriel was expanded over her entire person. One sensed an ardent gaze filtering through those dark lashes, on the alert, seeking in every man for the envoy of the Lord: the annunciator of the miracle of amour. The oval of her face was pure, the skin prettily amber-tinted. The design of her mouth was gracious and grave. She resembled Maya greatly, and yet the two sisters were only genuinely identical in the form of the nose and the arch of their eyebrows.

Morally, their characters had only one point of complete similarity. Both of them had the dogged, almost morbid faith in the Truth, with a capital T, that engenders fanatics. They were both believers! But they each had a different Credo.

As they pushed them gently toward the forest, the two grandmothers marched behind the young women, at the slow and rhythmic pace of nuns or priestesses.

....

....

....

Poker, manilla or bridge had followed the hunters' fine dinner. Pierre Montala and Louis Dubar had found ingenious pretexts for avoiding the Queen of Spades, and after having lost a few louis, Robert Dunant and Monsieur Montala went out to smoke a consolatory pipe. Without even consulting one another, the two friends walked toward the forest.

Why did they not go in the direction of the Plaine de l'Angelus, so calm, serene and airy? Because every man who has an enveloping taste for the softness that descends from heavy branches, and rises from a carpet of dead leaves, is invincibly drawn to the forest.

At Barbizon, the body seems to the seized by an irresistible magnet that emanates from the giant beech-trees and robust oaks. One believes that one is entering a cathedral of legend, and the sun itself only touches the ground beneath the foliage with the same discretion it exercises in piercing the most admirable Gothic stained glass. A lucidity compounded of calm and philosophy quickly dominates the conversations or reveries of strollers there. The mind soon opens up to all mystical enlightenment, because the vegetal magnetism exercises its benevolent magnetism on human nerves.

After a long silence, Robert Dunant said to his companion: "Will you permit me to find the love of your friend Madame Wiscorney for our old and beautiful forest excessive? It's not jealousy, but at her age, a woman is more suitably placed by her fireside than in the rocks. I trembled for her this morning. You ought to warn her about the danger of ricochets. One day, she'll be found dead after a hunt. Some maladroit poltroon will have killed her without meaning to."

"I've said all that to her," replied Montala, "but try to talk reason to the daughter of a Dalai Lama who thinks she's invested with a divine mission and has arrived at the age of white summits! She told me that she ought to have retired a year ago to a high mountain, to live among beasts and trees, in order to accomplish the final mutation of her soul."

"What are you talking about? So far as I know, only exceedingly rare Hindu sages risk such proofs? It's high time that the ascetics and the Christian cenobites renounced that petty game of grottos and caves without central heating."

"It is, however, the Promised Land of which that supremely intelligent and cultured woman dreams. Anyway, this is what she told me of her history...

....
....
....

"Madame Wiscorney has absolutely no idea from whose entrails she was born, or which mortal sowed the seed in the maternal womb. She believed herself for a long time to be the daughter of the Dalai Lama, who had found her in one of the bungalows that the Indian princes construct in the jungle to facilitate their tiger hunts. Those shelters also serve as refuges for strays and the belated. There is always a room at the disposal of a traveler in distress.

"One stormy day, the high priest was surprised by a tornado, and went into one of those so-called 'guestrooms.' Between two lightning-flashes he saw, in a corner of the shelter, a poor little creature half-dead of hunger and fear. As soon as he approached her, the child, who might have been a little over three years old, put her hands together and nestled in the lama's robe with such a tender confidence that he didn't have the heart to abandon her when the tempest had eased. He even waited there until the following day in case her parents returned—but no one came to find the child, and no one ever knew whether Monsieur le Tigre had devoured two imprudent spouses, or whether the abandonment was the crime of an unnatural mother.

"When one is the Dalai Lama, one is very powerful; one knows all the mysteries of magical science; is surrounded by Houtouktous, Panditas, Kampos, Maramabas and Mahatmas; but one is ignorant of the mysteries or puericulture.[4]

"Having no one in his service but young monks even more incompetent than himself, he entrusted Tussilia— which means 'the daughter of the bungalow'—to the gentlest and oldest of his scholars. He told him to make a Houtouktou of her—which is to say that he was to educate the child in the art of auguries, the science of trances and that of divine messages.

---

[4] The term "houtouktou," describing a kind of lama, was apparently first introduced to a French audience by Père J.-B. Du Halde's geographical account of China and Tartary, published in 1735; it crops up regularly thereafter in geographical texts and journalistic accounts of Buddhism and Tibet. A pandita is also a kind of Asiatic priest, but the other two terms in the list are either misappropriated or invented, initiating a pattern manifest throughout the text. I shall annotate those that play a significant role within the text for which I can identify existing meanings, but will let the improvised terms pass without comment.

"The caprice of fate determined that Tussilia was prodigiously endowed for that destiny. She learned very rapidly, and thoroughly, the sacred language that permitted her, while still a child, to read the rarest and most ancient manuscripts. To cut a long story short, one day, when she reached her fourteenth year, hazard put her in the presence of her savior, the Dalai Lama of Lhasa, and the holy man interrogated her. He was so amazed by her responses that he retired to his oratory and started searching through the prophetic scrolls, in order to see whether some great mission might have been promised to the Child of the Bungalow.

"Toward midnight, he found a script several thousand years old, which he deemed to apply to Tussilia. Madame Wiscorney has often recited the text to me, of which this is the tenor:

"To the priests that the spirits of the yellow race will inhabit will be sent, in the ozone of the lightning, a woman with bright eyes. She will bear on her right arm the mark of the ring with which Brahytina encircles the wrists of his elect. She will be ornamented by a perfect beauty, and her gaze will have the power to tame the white goros—which is to say, priests—*of the west. It will be necessary to instruct her with all the secrets of the genesis of the world, for she must live in the darkness of the Occident, so long as her flesh shall flourish. But as soon as the sacred lotus of her body is half-withered, in order to respire the azure of Brahma it will be necessary for her to sow the Acquired Truths in the minds of pale caterpillars. For the Redemption of peoples will be nigh and the promised Messiah will be born of the daughter of her daughter.*

"The very next morning, the Dalai Lama summoned Tussilia and asked her to show him her bare arms. The Marambas surrounding the high priest were able to observe that in fact, a kind of scar, like those left by second-degree burns, marked the young woman's forearm. I've seen the sacred sign, and it does resemble some kind of scar, but the doctors of theology in Lhasa declared unanimously that no doubt was any longer possible. The iron ring of the King of the World had definitely been secured in place there. It was in opening it to set her free that the spark of unknown Forces had burned the flesh of the pre-destined virgin.

"After a kind of scholarly examination, it was agreed that Tussilia would leave the convent of Lhasa and spend twelve months among the Taurens, and thirty-nine moons among the Parchment Dragons."

"What does that mean?"

"It means that she was to spend a year studying medicine and three years studying biology, geology and, above all, prehistoric verities."

"Can't they talk like anyone else, as MacNab would certainly say?"

"At sixteen, she knew by heart all the old texts sheltered from the air in glass bells and guarded by erudite and fanatical old monks. Bewilderingly, it appears that those men have the right to learn the verities of the Truth, but only on condition of voluntarily making it impossible for them to reveal it thereafter. In order not to succumb to the temptation of scything down the errors that pullulate in the world by speaking, they make a vow of exile. They go from one monastery to another, but always at a higher altitude. They never go near a valley. In the convents neighboring, or even confused with the eternal snows, they live on roots and water. They study, they learn what people would die to know, but never, once initiated, can they be forsworn.

"The man whose hunger for the unknown can no longer be sated by the monastery solicits from his superior one day his right to 'the step.' The doyen reminds him in detail of the harsh life that awaits him, but a being afflicted with ennui has even fewer ears than a hungry belly. After a blessing, he is given food and a map. With the stars for reference points and the thirst for science that preys upon him for sustenance he departs alone, never to return, along scarcely-traced tracks. He disappears.

"The man who does not die on the way arrives one day that he refuge he seeks. The door is always open. No one questions him. He responds to a few mute signs, and in the most profound silence. He is introduced into the room of the parchments. It appears that the greater the heights the monks attain in the mountains and Knowledge, the happier and more fulfilled they seem. Sincerity and joy are the recompense for those vain studies. I say 'vain' because, for centuries and centuries, they have not been of any service to humankind.

"Great was the amazement of the monks of Tibet to see the Daughter of the Bungalow arrive among them, but no one doubted her mission, and she lived among the saints, the monks assigned by the prophecy. I'll wager, however, that a long time after she had quit them, the memory of her beauty and her smile still made the sagest of the sage dream.

"All that she has revealed to me of her mysterious studies is that she has seen, with her own eyes, plans of aircraft, submarines and automobiles dating back fifteen thousand years before Jesus Christ. She claims that writing has been lost three times on the earth. Thought-reading, which marks one of the phases of human evolution, has existed before. However, arts of speech and writing then became useless, and the spoken word and the pen became obsolete. Fortunately for the loquacious, and for poets, the universal silence of humanity is always followed by the fatal cataclysm that accompanies the somersault of the being known as the Earth, hindered by its growth in its cocoon of humus. *Flic, floc!* A wave from the depths inundates the continents...and everything begins all over again..."

....

....

....

While chatting in that fashion, the two hunters had traveled along the Allée du Bas-Bréau and returned toward the village by a long curve through the woods, which finally brought them to the Chemin du Bornage. Robert Dunant was about to laugh at Madame Wiscorney's revelations when bursts of youthful laughter rang in his ears. He parted a honeysuckle bush and saw the uncommon spectacle of two men dressed for hunting playing tennis with two young women.

"I suspected as much," growled Montala. "Pierre hasn't held back. Look! In spite of the snobbery with which he's smitten, he's forgotten the nails in his shoes and is casually making a mess of the tennis court. No need to tell you why. He's in love with the blonde—and the cunning Dubar has had himself introduced to the brunette."

"Ha ha! If the twins are rich, two marriages might make the good fortune of four people."

"I wouldn't see any inconvenience in that, if Maya's husband weren't caught up, according to Madame Wiscorney, in the great drama of the Redemption of the World. He will, she says, be one of those who will bring, from air or fire, the necessary god or gods to the earth.

"Now, I don't want my son to be an aviator, or a mariner, or an explorer. He'll be a simple manufacturer, like his worthy father, and enjoy life. I don't trust people, myself. They've already killed one Messiah and martyred his apostles, in order to worship them later at their ease. Now, as all that has been successful before, they'll do it all over again for the next Redeemer. None of that for Pierre!"

"So you believe in the old Hindu woman's nonsense?"

"Does one ever know?"

"But tell me, what connection can there be between Madame Wiscorney and the Crazy Rock?"

"None. What are you thinking?"

"Nothing—I'm asking."

....

....

....

....

....

Everything that Monsieur Montala had said was perfectly true. Madame Wiscorney really was a foundling, and the Tibetan convents had delivered the oldest secrets in the world to her. The young Hindu had been seventeen when she took advantage of a torrid summer to descent from the last monastery, that of Kampa-Dzong, set at an altitude of five thousand meters on the slopes of Mount Everest.

She had lived on the sacred glacier for a year. Then she had separated, reluctantly, from the seven old and wise monks who had treated her as the predestined daughter—which is to say that they had worshiped her as the promised goddess of the decadent race. She had had the prescience, on leaving them, that the role that had been attributed to her was a trifle heavy for her pretty shoulders, but she did not show it, and her white silhouette, draped in a white robe, soon merged with the masses of immaculate snow that she had to cross over go around. A cloud enveloped her with its moist and icy softness. And at the monastery, silence resumed all of its majesty and eloquence—for it is the great educator of souls.

Tussilia marched for a long time in the solitude of rocks and forests. The animals watched her pass by, and an old python, blissfully digesting, even swayed its head to salute her.

After a month of traveling, she found herself prostrate at the feet of the Dalai Lama, in a mission at Tapchen. He blessed her, and brought her gently to her feet.

With him at the time, having come to talk international politics, was Lord Wiscorney, whom England had charged with circumventing the leader of the believers of Tibet. While the high priest and the young Hindu conversed in low voices, he abandoned himself to the charm of her exquisite presence. That day, Tussilia was wearing the gold lamé robe of the Taurens, disciples of Aliage-Nar. A broad jade bracelet hid the scar of the ring of Brahytina, and on a purple silk headband, a black triangle placed the seal of the Mahytmas.

Before taking her leave of her savior and the foreigner, the young woman fixed her gaze on that of the English diplomat. The latter went pale, was disturbed, and, involuntarily, took two steps toward the door after Tussilia.

No ambassador ever dragged out diplomatic negotiations for so long. And never, in Asiatic memory, had an Occidental been seen to study Buddhist theology with such ardor. It is necessary to add, too, that the Dalai Lama, having divined the passion that was burning Lord Wiscorney for the beautiful Initiate, did not hesitate to make use of that lure to obtain more from England than England wanted to accord to him. He interested the envoy in the mysteries of Temples, and gave him the child of the Bungalow for a guide.

After three months, literally enchanted, Horace Wiscorney asked for Tussilia's hand, and promised in exchange, in the name of his government, everything that the wily high priest of Lhasa wanted to obtain.

The predestined one was very surprised when the Marambas offered her, in the temple, with great ostentation, a kind of marshal's baton, handed to her by a short, stout Tachour. In the hollow of the bamboo there was a parchment scroll covered with wax seals and mysterious characters. Their purpose was to accredit the Initiate among the white goros who might dare to doubt her mission.

Afterwards, the Dalai Lama put the rings of engagement on the fiancée's fingers. He told her, weeping, that she was about to enter the darkness of the West predicted by the prophecy. She would marry the English ambassador, would go to live in the cold and the fog, in order to give enlightenment to a pale caterpillar. Death and tears would mark the required period of sacrifice, which would last forty-five years. Afterwards depending on the vigor of her strength, she would either return to Tibet in order to die there in the convent of the seven sages, or climb a nearby mountain in order to die there in accordance with the sacred rites.

Snow is the shroud of the true elect of God.

....
....
....
....
....

When the Dalai Lama fell silent, the temple emptied of its priests and its worshipers. Then Tussilia started to weep, as Christ wept in Gethsemane. But, for her as for him, the chalice was not taken away. The very next day, she tasted the bitterness of the first kiss that Lord Wiscorney placed on her mouth. No emotion caused her to part her lips under that caress.

In the company of the Lama of Lhasa, the English ambassador was a man of tall stature, impeccably correct attitude and perfectly distinguished. He was, however, incapable of resisting the two passions that haunted him: alcohol and beauty.

He was the widower of an exquisite Irishwoman, whom the sun of India had consumed in six weeks, and the most flattering flirtations had not consoled him. Only alcohol poured forgetfulness into him, and the waters of that Christian Lethe made of him, by the twentieth hour, a silent and stupid brute.

The marriage of the Initiate and the diplomat was the occasion for marvelous ceremonies and interminable feasts. In all religions, the ministers of God greatly appreciate the joys of the table; so, for at least a week, there was nothing but incense, liquor and good cheer. In accordance with Asiatic custom, Tussilia only participated in the preparation for the feasts, and as she was praying while her husband was drinking, she did not find any intoxication in the kisses reeking of whisky and gin that midnight brought her in the European's arms.

Then the day came when, enveloped in somber gauzes, she saw the Temple of Lhasa disappear over the horizon, and even the mauve line of the mountains where science had illuminated her soul forever.

With dry eyes, she watched the last white dot of the snows of Sakia vanish. It was as if the flame or a torch was extinguished within her then, and as if, henceforth, she would go through life like a blind person, stumbling at every step. Distress put a shadow so intense into her yellow-streaked eyes that Lord Wiscorney became anxious. Not knowing how to express himself, he said, in bad Hindi.

"I love you, my treasure!"

Then she half-smiled, and considered that man, whose benevolent egotism was unconcerned with the state of her soul, but thought that his own happiness would console all regrets.

"I love you, I love you," he repeated, at each of Tussilia's sighs.

Hieratic and glacial, she made no response to the three words of love, save for a slow and monotonous prayer;

"Om...om...mani hung."[5]

And her spouse never understood why she appealed for the help of God or the sacred lotus flower, at the moment when the Occidentals turn their icons to the wall.

....
....
....

Exile was propitious to Tussilia's beauty. She dazzled all those with whom she came into contact. And as she was soon made to learn the English language, to dress tastefully and to equal in tact the most highly-reputed ladies in the society of the Diplomatic Service, her success

---

[5] This is a version of the mantra nowadays conventionally rendered as *Om mani padmi hum*, the middle two words—which are really a portmanteau term—referring to the sacred lotus, and the final syllable, if it has any meaning other than an interjection, to wisdom or compassion.

increased her husband's passion. In fact, she incarnated worldly seduction and mystique in its most troubling charm.

In 1877 she gave birth to a daughter, whose health was never robust. However, without neglecting her duties as an ambassador's wife, she directed her child's education, and taught her a few of the secrets of which she was the custodian. They did not broaden the mind of the dainty Dolly, however, which was delightfully affectionate and banal. As the prophecy only concerned her granddaughter, Tussilia contented herself with being a mother, and forgot her title of Initiate.

Tussilia did not suffer at all when her husband's love diminished, until all conjugal duties ceased. She was devoid of anger as she was devoid of regret, and her serenity was so perfect that Lord Wiscorney finally understood that he had only ever possessed the body of the Daughter of the Bungalow.

He did not forgive her for the insult of having removed her heart and her sensuality. Masculine logic does not admit that a woman can exclude her soul or her senses from marital property. The alcohol-saturated gentleman considered himself a victim and an offended party, so he died in a London bar, with a bottle of whisky in his hand, while he was relating his sentimental misadventure to another no-less-distinguished drunkard.

....
....
....
....
....

When Dolly Wiscorney was requested in marriage by the seductive Maurice d'Angeville, Tussilia was very perplexed. Her future son-in-law's family was so intransigent in religious matters that she feared the worst quarrels for her child. She had raised her darling in the broadest tolerance, and the sole morality of duty and conscience. No confession counted her among its faithful. But love—as is often the case in its first access—held sway over the young woman's logic. Without hesitating for a second, she accepted the god that her Maurice worshiped, and received baptism amid two violent disputes—for Madame Wiscorney and Madame d'Angeville defended their convictions bitterly; one, in the name of Science, denied the Messiah Jesus, and the other, in the name of Faith, denied any truth that the Gospel did not mention.

While the fiancés abandoned themselves to the intoxication of dreams and kisses, the two mothers-in-law measured one another with the gazes full of challenge that boxers exchange before a title fight.

Maurice d'Angeville took his young wife to Paris. Tussilia followed her there.

As the awakening of certain psychic faculties warned the Daughter of the Bungalow that the hour of her mission was approaching, however, she resolved to prepare for it by means of the open-air exercises, immobility and prayer prescribed by the Houtouktous.

Forests are, in the opinion of all theosophies, reservoirs of magnetic force. It is sufficient for the exhausted to sit down with their backs to determined trees to be recharged with vital energy, like a battery whose salts are renewed. The Druidesses knew the magic of vegetable essences, and Solomon himself often experienced that of the Sycamore. The Initiate of the secrets of the Asiatic Om, of course, was not unaware of the special virtues of the magnetism of the oak, the beech, the pine and all the other branches that sway in a forest. A vegetable eats, drinks, respires, flowers, loves, suffers and dies. It is a being. It speaks, it reveals, it instructs, it soothes or it overexcites.

"To listen to the voice of a plane-tree," Buddha says, "is not only to hear the rustle of its foliage; it is necessary to lean forcefully against its bark, and to await the mysterious frisson that will unfailingly be born in the warmth of the human body, and the effluvia of the vegetal sap. When the contact is established, one suffers, to begin with, a malaise comparable to that engendered by the presence of a stranger whose language one does not speak, but gradually, the tenderness of a communion rises within us; a soul visits our soul, and the dialogue commences."

Now, every being condemned to remain, throughout life, within a narrow radius, has more leisure and strength to study what is happening around it. A tree lives two existences simultaneously: one in the darkness and the other in the light. It is necessary for it to struggle against all the elements, and it is prey to parasites issued from the darkness as well as those born in the light. Its roots are subject to the assault of the most sinister larvae, the ugliest and blindest beasts, and yet its spreads out, digging into the soil, in spite of the misery of mutilations, thirst and hunger. It clings to the earth, its mother and its nurse, aspires it, drains it pitilessly, and that for the sole sensuality of rising into the azure, of respiring the atmosphere of eagles, humans and gods. Deprived of wings and movements, it shivers nevertheless when a titmouse, leaping from branch to branch, cries the joy of its liberty. By night, it cradles everything that sings, chirps or coos. The spring, its lover, offers it, along with new pasture, the lesson of myriads of idylls.

It knows the emotion of swooning elytra, affectionate beaks, covered nests. From the fauna and the flora it knows so many things that our poor human anguishes are child's play for that impassive observer. The trees talk, and telepathy is their speech. By placing his back to olive-trees, Jesus drew the strength necessary to accept his martyrdom. He wept, and his divine tears fell upon the bark of a tree. The vegetal, that night, communed with the Christ, as the second precious infinity into which he exhaled all human sweetness and bitterness. When Jesus no longer had any human disciples, or friends, the trees offered him their energy and the consolation of their mystery. What a lesson!

Tussilia, therefore, searched for the forest most propitious to her psychic advancement. The forest of Fontainebleau, with its rocks, its silence and its high foliage, appear to her to combine all that was necessary for the encouragement of a superior mediumship. She searched for the spot with the best aura—which is to say, the one whose perfumes and effluvia were most sympathetic to her senses. She found that Barbizon responded to the demands of her Initiate exercises.

She bought a small villa, which seemed enlaced by the ultimate branches of the forest, and it was there that she lived for the nine months that separated her from her last and greatest dolor.

Disdaining the paths beaten by strollers, she was seen exploring the most deserted and most impracticable areas from the Gorge to Néfliers, from the Alpinists' path to the desert of Aprémont.

She emerged from her dwelling shortly after dawn and only went back at the extreme limit of dusk. Wild boar hunters and the members of the Club Alpin—those who like to scale certain blocks of sandstone that seem inaccessible—encountered her in the most solitary and least hospitable places. She seemed to be fond, however, of the chaos of rocks that bears the name of Cuvier-

Chatillon, and more than one gamekeeper was often bewildered to see her emerging close by, as if from a trapdoor. The escapades of the Crazy Rock began shortly after the Daughter of the Bungalow had made her temple in the forest, but no one noticed that coincidence, and the legend took form to the extent of pushing fools to make up stories as fantastic as they were dramatic.

....
....
....
....
....

One day in September, when squalls of wind and rain had even discouraged the foresters Tussilia was going home in her soaking and mud-stained dress when she saw her son-in-law walking angrily back and forth outside the front door of the Villa Ourton.

"Quickly! Quickly!" he shouted, as soon as he saw her. "Dolly's dying. Come on!"

Five minutes later, Maurice d'Angeville and his mother-in-law departed for Paris like a whirlwind.

"Dolly fell off a stool trying to get a book from my bookshelves," he said, between changing gear and letting out the clutch. "Two hours later she gave birth to twins. I don't know the technical name of the lesion caused by the fall, but the doctor affirms that she won't see another dawn. It's enough to drive one mad!"

Tussilia thought that her heart was about to break, but she did not weep, and isolated herself in a prayer so profound that the unhappy husband dared not trouble his mother-in-law's dolorous silence with a single word.

When they arrived at the young wife's bedside, Madame d'Angeville was holding the dying woman's hand. In the gap between the bed and the wall, in the same crib, two little pink and wrinkled beings were waving their little closed fists, and sucking an imaginary teat in their sleep.

"Mama!" Dolly murmured. And sobs filled the silence.

"My daughter, my darling...be strong! If you want to live, you'll live!"

"I can't want any longer; I can't do any more, Mama! I confide them to you...adieu!"

"No, *au revoir!*"

"Yes, that's true...you told me...thank you. I'm not afraid! My lovelies...give me my lovelies..."

With hands that were already diaphanous, the young mother caressed the two little girls, which had rapidly nestled into her arms. Then, in a voice that became weaker and weaker, she said: "Maurice! Maurice! I'm confiding them to Mama! Pray, pray, Mama! Vertigo... abyss... adieu!"

Death then broke the last filament that still retained the young soul to the bloodless body of the injured woman. Even the most highly-evolved Initiate cannot avoid the atrocious suffering of psychic detachment; for a moment, Tussilia was as pale as the cadaver of her daughter, and perhaps she would have shed perfectly legitimate tears if Madame d'Angeville had not suddenly cried: "Oh, my God, she's dead! And without absolution! Without a crucifix! Quickly, a rosary and holy water! Run and fetch a priest."

Then the Hindu stood up, as grave and hieratic as a priestess.

"Will you please cease all agitation, Madame. My child is no more, and her soul needs no prayer but mine."

"Sacrilege!" said the indignant Catholic.

"Truth," replied Tussilia. "Dolly knew enough for her departure to be devoid of fear. Her carnal vehicle has been accidentally broken; she must go to seek another in order to complete her course, but her mind had not been falsified by legends. She will be reincarnated, and will find her birth on the astral plane. Time is nothing, and cannot hinder the evolution of souls. Let us give to her form, which she modeled in the shadow of my entrails, the decent attitude that is appropriate to the nobility of death. First of all, let us replace my wards in their crib."

"Do you hear, my son? This woman is a heretic and insane. You're not going to confide the salvation of these two angels to her?"

"Shh! Not another word!" said the man addressed, in a sudden fit of fury.

Despair does not admit any harassment, nor distraction, and Maurice d'Angeville was, at that moment, so distressed by the misfortune that that had fallen upon him that he could not tolerate any noise. Kneeling down and leaning over the inert hand of his wife, he covered her with hectic kisses.

Tussilia took advantage of the imposed silence to place herself at the foot of the bed, her heels together, her arms extended and her eyes closed, in order to proceed with the incantation of spiritual Guidance. The younger the body dies, the more fervent and urgent the appeal needs to be, for the Guides, trusting in the norm of decease, only hold themselves alert when the magnetic linkages mature. Now, for Dolly, a tragic fatality had abruptly sheared her taut threads, and the soul was running the risk of a dangerous solitude in the darkness of the after-death.

The mother, an initiate, put so much ardor into seeking the anxious shade of her child that her body suddenly emitted iridescent light. A kind of blue mist emerged from her throat, which became yellow as it rose toward her forehead. Mauve effluvia extended from her fingers, and that radiation was so intense that Madame d'Angeville conceived a vague fear in consequence.

"Look, Maurice—she's burning! She's a demon!" she said.

"It's miraculous, Mother! She's not burning—she's shining like a saint!"

"We need to throw holy water over her!"

"I'd rather call to her softly. *Belle-Maman? Maman?*" he said.

Tussilia shuddered, lowered her arms and let herself slide to the floor, in the desolate attitude of Bartholomé's *La Pleureuse.*[6] Even though he hid her face in her hands, multitudes of tiny violet and yellow sparks fulgurated over her entire silhouette.

"Belle-Maman! Maman!" repeated the poor widower.

Then, a trigger was released within Madame Wiscorney, whose eyes opened, and finally allowed the tears to flow.

"Let's take care of her clothing now," she said, finally.

....
....
....
....
....

Without taking off their crepe veils, the two women, when they returned from the cemetery, leaned over the cradle at the same time. Each one took one of the baby

---

[6] A gilt-bronze statuette by Albert Bartholomé (1848-1928), produced in an edition of several hundred, also reproduced in ivory, and in stone, as a funerary monument, including one example on the grave of Henri Meilhac. In consequence, it became a very familiar image.

girls in her arms. Maya, who had held out her little arms to Tussilia, immediately received the pagan baptism of dolor, for two large tears fell upon her forehead, emerged from the Initiate's eyes. Madame d'Angeville, for her part, hugged Ghislaine and melted.

"Poor little orphans!" she said, sobbing.

The father came in as the two grandmothers were replacing the children in their crib.

"You heard my daughter's wish," sad Madame Wiscorney, simply. "I shall keep my promise. First of all, I shall take the twins to Barbizon."

At those words, Madame d'Angeville burst forth in imprecations, affirming that her son would be excommunicated if he compromised the salvation of the two souls that Heaven had confided to him.

An argument of unusual violence, such as can only arise within families, followed that declaration. After a quarter of an hour of patience, Madame d'Angeville, driven to excess, wishing to reconcile her conscience and filial respect, cut short the debate by means of a judgment in the manner of Solomon; it was agreed that each of the two grandmothers would bring up one of the granddaughters as she pleased.

The two human larvae, who were sucking their fists while their destiny was regulated, discovered from the next day on that they no longer had the same guardian angel. Ghislaine was obliged to seek her life in a warm and sterilized feeding-bottle, while Maya slaked her thirst at the smooth and swollen breast of a Berrichonne nurse.

The raising of the two babies, even though it was effectuated in diametrically opposite conditions, had the most fortunate results. The perfect health of the two sisters permitted them to grow up in grace and beauty. It would have greatly embarrassed the father if he had been obliged to declare which of his two daughters was the prettier and the more robust.

When they reached their fifth year, however, he demanded that the two grandmothers reunite the twins for a fortnight every year. So long as he did not remarry, that encounter would take place under his roof.

....

....

The first time that Ghislaine and Maya saw one another they were infinitely pleased with one another, took one another by the hand and went to sit down together in a corner of the paternal study, in order to exchange their infantile secrets. It was adorably charming. First, they offered one another the toys that their little hands were clutching, and each one contemplated the object lent to them.

After a long silence they recovered their respective toys and questioned one another.

"Who gave you your doll?"

"It was Petit Noël," said Ghislaine.

"It was my Lia who bought my little bear." That was what she called her grandmother; in her little brain, that signified *Mama Tussilia*. "Who is Petit Noël?" she asked, intrigued.

"It's Jesus—you know Jesus?"

"No, I don't."

"You don't know Jesus? The little good God, who comes down the chimney and puts gifts in your stocking?"

"Don't know."

"Then…who do you ask for what you want?"

"My Lia."

"Me, Jesus."

"Have you seen him?"

"No."

"Then how do you know it's him?"

There was a second's hesitation and silence. "Because Mémé says so," said Ghislaine, cutting the argument short.

The next day, there was another subject of perplexity for Maya. Her sister, after having played orange-seller, sat down, exhausted, on the carpet. They had both eaten and sold so many golden fruits in their imagination that they were tired and full.

"What are you thinking about, Maya?" said Ghislaine. "The beauty in the dormant wood?"[7]

"She isn't sleeping at Barbizon."

"Of course! Petit Poucet, then? Cinderella, or Donkey-Skin's beautiful dress?"

"Who are those ladies?"

"Doesn't anyone tell you nice stories? Don't you know what a fairy is?"

"No."

"She's a princess with a magic wand, who does things…things…anyway, who does anything you want her to."

"Oh. My Lia mustn't know any. I've never seen one."

"Nor have I."

"Then how do you know it's true?"

"Mémé told me, I tell you!"

Maya returned to Barbizon with her mind dazzled by all the marvelous things her sister had told her. So, as soon

---

[7] I have translated the title of Perrault's classic tale accurately rather than using the conventional English substitute ("The Sleeping Beauty"), in order that Maya's reply makes sense, but I have substituted the familiar English equivalents where it has no effect on the surrounding text.

as the maid had taken off her coat, the scamp ran to sit on the stool at Tussilia's feet. Leaning on the old lady's knees, the series of questions commenced: "My Lia, do you know Noël? The bogey man? The ogre? Cinderella? And the Fairy Godmother?"

"No, my child."

"Then you don't know anything!"

"I know everything that's true, my darling, but I don't see any point in making fun of you. I want you to trust me and I never lie to you, because nothing is as vile as lying, even to be pleasant. Your sister is a lovely child, but people deceive her. It's her grandmother who buys her toys; Noël doesn't exist. Nor the bogey man! Nor fairies!"

"Oh, what a pity!" said the child, desolate at no longer being able to hope for miracles from a slender magic wand."

"My darling, it's necessary not to expect more from life than it can give. Now go to bed; obey my voice and not fear. There is no ogre, no werewolf, and if there are malevolent forces in the world, you'll learn their names later.

"Why, my Lia?"

"Because the Truth can't be understood by little girls."

"It has no magic wand, the Truth? It doesn't give you beautiful dresses the color of the moon?"

"No, my love, on the contrary—but it's so beautiful that you'll love it anyway. Go on, good night."

An hour later, her little body scarcely emerging from the bedclothes, Maya was asleep. Her regular breath, the calm of her features and the warmth of her skin attested that the carnal envelope was in a perfect state, and was resting from the fatigues that the soul, absent for a few hours, had imposed on it. A nightlight cast little dancing gleams over the warm scene, which seemed to be battling with somber and fearful beings.

Tussilia appeared in the doorway then. She was straight and simple in her black dress, and her muffled footfalls did not awaken any echo. She approached the bed, stood still for a few minutes, and then, placing her finger on Maya's head between the eyes and the middle of the forehead, she said in a whisper:

"Pretty little soul, efface from the cells of that brain all the nonsense written therein during the vacation. You can see, at this moment, that those lies are cluttering up the field of your spiritual vision uselessly. Efface, efface! Good! Tomorrow, to recompense you, the forest will give you your first lesson. Listen to your Guides until dawn. Adieu!"

Then Tussilia disappeared into the hole of shadow that marked the entrance to her bedroom.

....
....
....

As soon as she got dressed in the morning, Maya displayed a few impulses of indiscipline. Several times, she said to her grandmother: "Ghislaine doesn't do that; why should I?"

"Because it's necessary."

"And if I didn't, what would happen?"

"You'd be committing a fault, whose consequences I couldn't spare you."

"What's a fault? What's a consequence?"

"The forest will teach you. Hurry up, darling. Bring your study book."

It was the fifteenth of June. The insects, which take their delights in rocky terrains, were hastening to their nesting. The burrowers, winged or not, were scratching the thin layers of sand that the wind had lodged between two stones, preparing cradles for the little families whose hatching they would not see. In the meantime, the caterpillars of imminent butterflies were stuffing themselves on the tender leaves of nearby plants. They scissored ardently and fattened themselves methodically

Maya, trotting and playing, ran ahead of her grandmother along the paths that go from the Grand Majoré to the viewpoint at the Camp du Chailly. She turned round continually, asked a question, without expecting an answer, and set off again at a run. They both arrived in that fashion on the familiar plateau, from which the gaze can embrace kilometers of the plain. From there, everyone can evoke in the imagination all the regiments of French guards, hussars or musketeers that Louis XIV watched maneuvering in that area.

Sitting in a corner of the meager verdure that cushions the stony soil of that crossroads in a miserly fashion, Maya opened her book and Tussilia began to meditate. Instead of concentrating on the text to be learned, however, the little girl's mind went with her gaze from the branch of a bramble to a heather root, to leap immediately to a wild strawberry and pause on a columbine. Suddenly, the child uttered a cry, in which disgust, fear and interrogation were combined.

"What is it?" said Madame Wiscorney, hastily abandoning the mysterious confines of the Infinite in which she took refuge during the slightest silence.

"Oh, look my Lia! All the leaves of that strawberry plant are covered in caterpillars, but because they're as green as the leaves, you don't see them right away."

"Yes, nature colors them in that fashion to protect them from their enemies. It's called mimicry."

"Well, I wouldn't like to resemble what I eat, and if I were them I'd do what this one is doing…look…she's left her sisters and she's eating that flower! How pleasant her meal must be! She's feeding on blue velvet and mauve satin!"

"Uh oh, how imprudent! What a fault she's committed…"

"A fault! A fault! But what's a fault?"

"You'll see, and understand the reason for obedience. Watch. Look…do you see that beautiful insect with iridescent wings that's zigzagging through the air. It's called a spiny *Ammophila*.[8] Don't look at anything else except those two creatures: a drama is in preparation."

Two seconds later, in fact, the insect had cleaved through the air and fallen upon the caterpillar, whose emerald green stood out against the pale blue of the flower. The aggressor straddled its victim, which she bit behind the head, taking advantage of each of its shudders to plunge a sting into its segments. At every thrust, a part of the body was immobilized, expertly paralyzed by the liquid that its executioner was injecting.

"Oh, the wicked fly!" said Maya, desolate.

"Shh! At this moment, your caterpillar is expiating the fault of independence that she committed, and her disobedience of the laws of nature."

Without paying any heed to the humans watching her, the wasp, after having shaken and smoothed her wings, resumed straddling her prey. In that martial position, it seemed natural that with a vigorous thrust, she was about to carry away that vanquished creature by the aerial

---

[8] *Ammophila* is a genus of wasps, commonly known as sand wasps. It is not obvious what the adjective *hérissée* [spiny or bristly] means in this context; it does not come from Fabre.

route. Not at all: with the inevitable awkwardness of an animal for whom walking is not the usual mode of loco-motion, the victorious insect began dragging the meal back to her young.

"How imprudent!" said Tussilia. "Another fault, gross in consequences."

At the same instant, an agile gray lizard bounded up-on the picturesque haulier and nearly took entire posses-sion of it. The insect owed her salvation to the rapidity with which she took flight. But the caterpillar bartered by force was destined to provide the newcomer with an *hors-d'oeuvre*. The genteel reptile blinked as it swallowed, and set about digesting it on a warm stone in the sunlight.

"Well, Maya? Do you understand what a fault is, and a consequence?

"Oh, yes," said the child, with a sigh. "But it's not fun to live, then, if it's necessary always to be good."

"The forest has given you the promised lesson, you see, my dear. When you've read a great deal, listened and understood, you'll find, in the contrary, that life is beauti-ful and goodness pleasant. Enough gravity for today— let's to home and you can play."

Such was the method that Tussilia employed to make her granddaughter a good girl, with an open mind, exer-cised in logic. The forest was Maya's School, while await-ing the time when it would become her Church.

....
....
....
....
....

Monsieur d'Angeville interrupted his widowhood when Ghislaine and Maya entered their eleventh year. His second wife, being scarcely twenty, was delighted not to have to occupy herself with the education of the twins. They were, however, brought to the wedding celebrations, and as the word "love" was frequently pronounced, Maya did not fail, on her return to interrogate her grandmother.

"Ghislaine told me that love is the Master of the world. She read it in a magazine, and heard it repeated seriously."

"No, not the Master, but the untamed and indispensable slave."

"Ghislaine introduced me to her lover—he's a schoolboy who kisses her in secret, gives her a little barley-sugar and forbids her to talk to some of his fellows. Grandmother d'Angeville doesn't know anything about it, and the joy of the secret makes my little sister blush."

"That's not love my child. That's a whim of instinct becoming manifest."

"But why is Papa going to sleep with his new wife?"

"In order to sow life in her."

"Life is sown?"

"Absolutely—like wheat and flowers."

"Was I sown?"

"Indeed."

"Ghislaine told me that we were found under a rosebush."

"That's not true. It was your Papa who sowed you in your mother's entrails."

"Well, how did I grow?"

"Oh, like a little plant. You know how vegetables grow and flower? Well, you did the same. You lived nine months to the detriment of your mother's flesh, you took from her blood, her muscles, her strength and her beauty, and then, when you were big enough, you came into the world, crying and weeping."

"Then mothers are the soil of little children?"

"Something like that, yes."

"How beautiful it is! That's what love is then?"

"Almost. At least, it's the sacred part of everything the word means."

....
....
....

From that day on, the word Love acquired, on the child's lips, the mystical and scientific sense that it truly has in nature. She no longer pronounced it except with a sort of respect, and with the aid of her young imagination, she had delicious words to express the labor of her thought. One evening, for example, as she was gazing at the firmament constellated with scintillations, Tussilia asked her:

"What do you think the stars are, child?"

"The seeds of the moon," she relied, without hesitation. "But what I say to myself, exactly, is that a seed always contains life, doesn't it? So, they're a lot of little moons that are waiting to be sown. Is the love that will make them hatch out the same as the love that caused me to be born?"

"Absolutely the same, for the Finite and the Infinite."

"What is the Papa of the stars called?"

"Om—the God of gods. Go to bed; the dew is settling on the earth to slake the thirst of your garden, and it's necessary not to catch cold."

....
....
....

While Maya departed for the land of dreams, the Daughter of the Bungalow went back inside, and in the obscurity of her bedroom she performed the exercise of Provision. That is the name given, in the School of Fakirs and Houktoutous, to a kind of mental concentration combined with certain gestures of physical gymnastics. The great Evolved, during these tiring frolics, populate the darkness with magnificent fulgurances. They draw gleams from the magnetic forces scattered around them analogous to those that one observed in laboratories when high tension electricity is established.

When Tussilia sensed that she was saturated with energies, she sat down on the floor, in the manner of Buddhas and prayed.

Suddenly, an unexpected prodigy brought her upright, breathless, literally drunk; a blinding light, with which the most powerful lighthouse cannot stand comparison, sprang from the exterior air and filled the frame of the French windows. In the midst of that dazzle, a form took shape, bright, transparent and gigantic.

Madame Wiscorney ran on to her balcony, and saw that immense form, floating and giving the impression of being made of clouds, like the Jupiter that Correggio depicted in his painting of the nymph Io.

The old Hindu extended her joined hands in front of her and bowed.

"O Kacyapa,[9] aged sage among Sages, have you come to punish me or instruct me?"

"To instruct you," murmured the impalpable Master.

---

[9] The Hindu Kacyapa, more frequently rendered Kasyapa, is one of the Seven Sages of the present universal cycle. He is credited with the authorship of the *Kashyapa Samhita*, a key reference text of Ayurvedic medicine, dealing in particular with gynecology and pediatrics. He is also credited in some texts with being the father of the divine Gardua bird, and in others with being the father of humankind, although those suggestions cannot apply to his role in the present text.

A sudden gust of wind curbed all the trees of the forest at that precise moment. Forces whistled through the branches, shaking the oldest trunks and making all the animals in their lairs quiver in fright.

That was the work of the elementals charged with ensuring the solitude of the Master. Their exploits are not always intelligent, for they are irritated by the terror to which they give rise. Their role is comparable to that of terrestrial dogs, and they guard the great Genii fluidically. The Asiatics, even the most evolved, fear them like starving dogs. In Europe the sylvan elementals are still very numerous and very active, and one encounters them in the Cévennes and the Pyrenees, never in the valleys but often in the vicinity of mountain paths.

So, Kacyapa, whom the Lamaists claim to be able to direct the causes of the great movements of humankind, smiled at the Initiate, who was kneeling down, listening to him.

"You asked the Spirit of the Rocks, a few days ago," he said, "what is the purpose of your mission. This is it, for you have omitted nothing of your science in the Instrument that has been confided to you. You merit the encouragement of my blessing. Maya, as you know, is to be the first vibration of the great cycle of Redemption. Artificial wings will lead to the wings of Genii. The ovipares will triumph over the vivipares, as equilibrium and the alternation of forces requires.[10] But in order for the

---

[10] I have conserved the terms "ovipares" and "vivipares" from the original text. They do not correspond to the classification of vertebrates into "oviparous" and "viviparous" species employed in modern biology, but have special meanings in a far more exotic system of classification, of which Tussilia will shortly offer an elaborate account.

reptation[11] of the mystical spiral to take place in light and in peace, it is necessary to overthrow of gods without burning their altars; it is necessary to annihilate all the books of the dead civilizations, because they weigh down souls and prevent them from rising up toward the light. Clear away! Clear away! Overturn! Combat! Form the new virgin, conscious and charming; but also form the new man. He will come; you will recognize him because he will be able to decipher the message that you will write for him, in order to bring him to your temple, and that in the imagistic style of Brahma! Blood, fire, iron and poison will envelop the predestined couple, which you will bring together; but you will vanquish, my sister! Do not forget that the love without darkness, the sublime and pure love, the love that creates superior forms, and will render to the ovipares their natural wings, will be reanimated on earth by the Initiate in the heart of the eagle and the devastating flight."

Tussilia raised her head in order to ask the Master a question, but no sound could emerge from her throat, which was paralyzed, as if she had seen Medusa.

Kacyapa was still smiling at her, but behind his white silhouette a colossal black and mocking shadow rushed toward the Sage. Then, racing through the forest with a tempestuous racket, the elementals interposed themselves.

---

[11] I have conserved the word "reptation," although its recent adaptation into English in the jargon of chemistry only gives it an analogical meaning, with respect to polymeric molecules; its literal meaning refers to the movement of snakes, especially when present in numbers and slithering over and beneath one another, which gives a better sense of the metaphorical meaning attached here to the evolution of the "mystical spiral."

There was a terrible battle of aerial currents; the house was shaken from its foundations to its roof; two shutters were torn from their hinges and broken tiles were scattered. As the bewildered Tussilia raised her eyes in order to defend herself by prayer, however, she saw the giant luminous ellipse that was carrying Kacyapa floating gracefully away, hastily disappearing toward the zenith.

When Maya came to embrace her grandmother the following morning, a slight disturbance invaded her. Nevertheless, she applied two sonorous kisses to the old lady's icy cheeks, saying: "Oh, my Lia, you're almost as white as the dress that you refused me in a dream last night."

....
....
....
....
....

It was eleven o'clock in the morning when Monsieur d'Angeville's automobile stopped in front of the Villa Ourton. He was accompanied by his young wife, his mother and a priest, a friend of the family. Tussilia reserved her most amiable welcome for the newcomers, and had a delicate meal prepared to celebrate the reunion.

She knew that a violent assault was about to be mounted on her, but she did not allow any sign of it to appear. She merely said, as they were about to sit down at the table: "Go have lunch at Madame Broca's house, my darling; I've warned her by telephone. You ought not to take part in the conversation that is going to render this lunch memorable."

At these words, the guests looked at one another, a trifle disconcerted. The priest considered the Initiate, who smiled at him benevolently, and invited him with a simple gesture to go into the dining room. As no one could decide to speak about the subject that was on their mind, Tussilia, as soon as the first course was served, declared in her most amenable tone: "It's a matter of a white dress, isn't it, Monsieur le Curé?"

"Yes, Madame," said the priest. "It isn't possible any longer to make the twins follow such opposed spiritual paths. They ought to worship the same God."

"But aren't you aware, Monsieur, that there is only one?"

"Yes—ours."

"Maya also knows that there is only one. The mystical point of departure of the two sisters is thus the same."

"What name does she give to the Omnipotent?"

"Om—which signifies God."

"Why don't you take her to Church?"

"Because the forest is sufficient for her. I can assure you that she learns to love life there and venerate the Supreme Master."

"What religion are you teaching her?"

"None."

"Why?"

"Because, all religions being excellent, I shall allow her to choose later the one that best corresponds to her taste as an accomplished nymph. If my Dolly had been raised in Protestantism, like her father, or Buddhism, like her mother, Maurice d'Angeville would never have married her—whereas, being free to accept the confession of the man she loved, there was no obstacle to her happiness."

"By what right to you interfere, Madame, in hindering the selection of souls?"

"By what right, Monsieur, do you impose a religion on the incarnate spirit when it cannot choose, being unable to discern?"

"The wisdom of the Church has decided that matter."

"I respect wisdom in all its manifestations, but I do not confuse it with Science. Dead religions, like living ones, are all echoes of the great verities of history and prehistory. Sacred science will be Maya's prerogative. Knowing that, she will understand all the Catholic, Jewish and other mysteries, and if it pleases her, one day, to inscribe herself in the Golden Book of one confession or another, at least it will be with a knowledge of the reason."

"You have, Madame, the pretention to explain the mysteries, while we, the ministers of God…?"

"Yes, Monsieur. The original task, redemption, communion, death, life, heaven, hell…all of that is clear and limpid. There is no mystery, there are only ignorant people."

"Arrogant woman, whom the demon of heresy possesses, we have come today to snatch from you the soul that you are damning."

"Priest devoid of light, know that one cannot struggle against certain forces."

"Will you, yes or no, allow Maya to take her first communion?"

"No—at least, not before she knows how certain magnetic currents lead to the divine centers."

"What is this gibberish?"

"The Truth, Monsieur."

"Enough stupidities," yapped Madame d'Angeville, suddenly. "Maurice wants Maya to kneel at the same Holy Table as her sister on the same day."

"I oppose that."

"In that case," exclaimed the father, mute until then, "I'm taking my daughter away immediately. Have her fetched, or I'll go and do it myself."

Tussilia did not flinch, but, with her eyelids closed, she crossed her hands over her throat. Immediately, Maurice, who had pushed back his chair and half-risen to his feet, began to tremble, and, his eyes staring into space, said in a fearful tone mingled with joy: "My Dolly..."

A frisson ran through the flesh of all the witnesses of that scene, and the maid was frightened.

A dialogue of which only one voice could be heard was immediately engaged.

"My Dolly, what have I done, then...?

"..."

"That's true...I promised..."

"..."

"No violence will be done to her!"

"..."

"That's sworn. But...am I the victim of a dream?" Maurice said, sponging his forehead.

"No, a hallucination!" exclaimed the priest.

"Well?" said the old Hindu woman, paler than death, after a silence. "Are you taking Maya away?"

"No...no," Maurice stammered.

Then, a sudden intense anger brought the minister of God to his feet. As he believed sincerely that he was dealing with an instrument of Beelzebub, he marched toward Tussilia, crucifix in hand.

"In the name of Christ and the Eternal Father, I command you to quit the body of this woman," he said to the imaginary demon.

Latin words flowed from his lips, and, excited by his own error, he pronounced the Christian exorcism, which, according to the holy canon, has the power to liberate the possessed.

Still calm and smiling, Tussilia stared at him intensely.

Suddenly, dominated by the hypnotic force of the Initiate's gaze, the priest was immobilized, his entire body extended in a dramatic attitude.

The young Madame d'Angeville was shaken by a nervous crisis, and Maya's paternal grandmother ran off in search of an ecclesiastic. Maurice, still distressed by the apparition of his first wife, was repeating untiringly: "It's enough to drive one mad! It's enough to drive one mad!"

After a few minutes, however, a measure of reason refreshed all their minds, and, still smiling, Tussilia said, tranquilly: "Shall we continue with lunch?"

"Where's my mother-in-law?" asked the young woman, suddenly pulling herself together.

"Here she is," said Madame Wiscorney.

Madame d'Angeville, looking crestfallen, was indeed coming back from a panic-stricken run through the garden. She had not been able to get through the garden gate.

As for the priest, his limbs curbed and his gesture discouraged, he returned the crucifix to his waist, and sat down meekly opposite his enemy.

"Madame," he said, with a sob in his voice. "You are the devil!"

"Come on—the devil is a creature of God, is he not? He can't be more powerful than his creator, or he would be God himself. A truce on obsolete words and futile discussions. Maya will take her first communion when she desires to do so, and she will do that when her soul has reached the stage of divine respiration. Then, she will need the divine, as she now has a hunger and thirst for matter."

"But why not prepare…?" the priest attempted.

"A parody? Or a rehearsal? But a parody isn't a preparation. I'm not criticizing anything; I'm not mocking anything; I demanded the freedom to model a soul; it was accorded to me. Every attempt at retraction on that point will engender psychic phenomena whose just consequences I cannot avoid."

Appetite not being concomitant with emotions of that sort, the guests only had one purpose, which was to quit that dwelling haunted by forces and phantoms. Even the aroma of a delicious coffee did not retain the two men, and when the engine of the auto purred in the road, everyone hastened to camouflage themselves as an inquisitor or a mummy—for the tourists, dressed for an excursion, were reminiscent of rebarbative silhouettes of the Middle Ages or the sarcophagi of Egyptian crypts.

....
....
....

A few months later, Ghislaine having accomplished the Eucharistic rites of the First Communion, was photographed in the white dress and veil that had enveloped her on the great day. Her forehead ringed with roses, her eyelids lowered and her hands joined, her image was reminiscent of angels or the blissful. Her childish beauty was idealized by the mystic gravity with which she had striven to realize the fiery words that she had been made to hear. Divine love had promised her spiritual ecstasy via the communion, and one sensed that all of her young and naïve body was still awaiting the sacred vibration.

It was moving and pure, as only great human hopes can be.

When Maya received the photograph of her sister she looked at it for a long time, and then began to weep. Tussilia pretended not to see that juvenile chagrin, and did not even raise her eyes when the girl said: "Oh, my Lia, I would have been pretty too in that white dress. Why did you refuse it to me?"

"Because you're not yet able to understand its meaning or its beauty."

"Am I more stupid than Ghislaine, then?"

"No. She doesn't know any more than you do, and you have only to question her to convince yourself of her ignorance."

In order to mark her triumph more clearly, and to tempt Maya with the propaganda of regrets, Madame d'Angeville came to Barbizon to spend the days of rest necessary to new communicants. The exercises of the Retreat had exhausted her.

As soon as the ears of the old ladies were at a respectable distance, Maya said to her sister: "I would have liked to be dressed like you. You wrote to me that grace had touched you, and the divine love had set you ablaze with its fire. Is that true?"

"Of course—I'm not a pagan, me!"

"And you were happy? Supernaturally happy, you told me? What does that divine happiness do to your head and your heart?"

"Huh? It doesn't do anything."

"What? It doesn't make you very hot or very cold? It isn't dizzying?"

"No. Anyway, I'm going to tell you a big secret. I think I'm a spiritual cripple, because I was listening to what the priest was saying, and I prayed and waited, closing my eyes...well, don't tell anyone, but I didn't feel anything—neither the grace, when it touched me, nor the divine love when it burned me. Shhh! It's a great disappointment, which I'm hiding from Mémé, because she thinks I'm an elect."

"On the contrary, it's necessary to tell her. Since she feels the presence of God, she'll help you to find it. Perhaps it passed you by."

"No, since it entered into me."

"But you didn't feel anything?"

"Nothing."

"Ah. Well, really, that doesn't astonish me, because, since terrestrial love is a sowing, divine love must be one too. I'll bet that you have to wait for the seed of the host to germinate inside you. But why didn't my Lia let God sow it in me? I'll ask her this evening."

....
....
....

Tussilia smiled maliciously when Maya told her about Ghislaine's mystical disappointments; but when her ward expressed the keen desire she had to know divine love as well, she became serious again and simply said: "That's all right, my child; we'll begin the sacred studies tomorrow."

At eight o'clock the following day, she took Maya to the ferns of Arbonne and told her why the cryptogams—which extend from algae to fungi and ferns—bear the astral signature of Saturn. It was the first time that she had employed the term "astral signature" and introduced the name of a planet into an explanation of the act of vegetal love.

"There are, you see," she said, "male ferns and female ferns, but the organs of reproduction escape human comprehension to such an extent that that obscurity causes them to enter the class of beings influenced by Saturn.

"Saturn, as you know, is one of the seven planets that weigh upon the destiny of everything that lives down here, stone, flower or animal. And in the domain of astrology—and I mean astrology, and not astronomy—it designs the earth. The fern was one of the first vegetables to be born of the famous primal clay of which all the holy books speak. And the spark of life that stood up first in the form of a cross, and then displayed itself in cut-out green leaves, still retains the secret of its origin. That mystery constitutes the distinctive sign, the signature. We'll probably never know from what hymen the Saturnians issued. We live on the cocoon of the Being of Fire that has been increasing and growing for centuries. It's nourished by the water of the sea, which is both its amniotic fluid and the plasma of all warm-blooded beings. When it began its metamorphosis, it exuded cells that were no longer necessary to it, but those cells retained in potency all the forces of life. They're what furnished the atoms indispensable to the birth of forms.

The scholars of the first ages called it"—she sketched a symbol[12]—"which is to say, Saturn, the future star, but it's confused today with the planet that bears the same name and is distinguished from the others by the luminous rings that encircle it."

"That's a funny sign. It looks like a letter *h* or a natural clef."

---

[12] The astrological symbol of Saturn has various modified forms, sometimes resembling a lower-case h with a crossbar on the upright, and sometimes a cross with a tail attached to the bottom curved like a question mark (hence Maya's comparison to a natural clef). Tussilia appears to be suggesting that the planet Saturn is merely a kind of positional marker for a more mysterious and active "astrological Saturn," and that the same is true for the other astrological entities that determine earthly evolution according to a purposive pattern. It is worth bearing in mind, when considering her invented astrology, that the astrological symbols for Mars and Venus are also used in biological science as the symbols for male and female, although, in her schema, "men" are not originally "from Mars" nor "women" originally "from Venus."

"It signifies: *that which is on high is similar to that which is below*. The important verity to retain, my child, is that all the Saturnians were and are still viviparates—which is to say that they emerge from animal forms in the state of mobile larvae. Today, they're primarily designated by the name of 'males.' But all the first beings were to the terrestrial nymph what the brand is to the fire, what warm ash is to the flame: a debris, a residue. They can only ignite ephemeral torches. And the glimmers will go out one day, in a supreme sputter, which will doubtless be the cry of agony of the Animal vanquished by the Elemental."

"Why isn't everything that moves dependent on Saturn?"

"Because, as the Earth emerged gradually from the waters, it described a slow ellipse that placed it, for a long time, under the action of various stars. Those modified, over time, the ephemeral beings subject to their radiation."

"Oh, all that's very difficult to understand, grandmother!"

"What? When the moon still attracts the water of the sea twice a day, it seems to you to be impossible that other planets weren't once able to weaken or fortify beings much more sensitive than a salty liquid mass?"

"That's true, my Lia."

"The astral influence that once lasted for three thousand years only acts today for thirty-three years."

"What force succeeded that of Saturn, then?"

"Jupiter. It was while it influenced the earth that the mud, the dust, the air and the waves were populated by the gigantic animals whose form and proportions science reconstitutes as best it can. Of the largest, having failed to resist the proof of the centuries, one only finds in ice and clay the last and much diminished examples of a few species. The Jupiterians, like the Saturnians, emerged alive and capable of nourishing themselves from their mother's breast.

"And did humans exist then?"

"Yes—but nothing permitted the anticipation of their present form. The sign of Jupiter is like a Z.[13] When you find it in an ancient text, you'll know what it signifies. The trees whose life can extent to a thousand years are of Jupiterian origin."

"What came after Jupiter?"

"The Moon, which presided over the modifications of the sea, the rivers and lakes. Under its influence, harmful to human industries, the waters were displaced and the terrestrial cocoon was raised up further above the waves. It was an epoch both sinister and poetic, in which beings endowed with movement were all gray, like seals, elephants and the hippopotamus. On the other hand, aquatic plants took on a pale green hue, which they still retain. Lunar beings are all ovipares. Many fish are lunar, as are the amphibians, a few herbaceous species and a few humans.

"Humans?"

"Yes—we'll return to that subject another day. The Moon is magnetic, and many minerals are classified under its signature."

"What came after the blonde Moon?"

"The Sun. And then commenced the terrible struggle for existence between two enemy species: the vivipares

---

[13] The original text presumably uses a Z because the typesetter had no way to reproduce the complex astrological symbol for Jupiter, which is supposedly symbolic of the Jupiterian thunderbolt (lightning) or eagle—both of which analogies are drawn at times by Dulac's text—and thought a Z most closely akin to the zigzag of lightning.

and the ovipares. Under the action of its light and heat, eggs were able to hatch, and the individuals that were hatched multiplied to the point that the Saturnians nourished themselves on them exclusively. They were forced to do that, in fact, because the metals, whose half-baked clay they liked, were hardened by desiccation. The age of purées of gold or silver was over, and the change of diet transformed the habits of those that survived. Nine tenth of precious stones are solar."

"And humans?"

"Humans—which is to say, the beings from which your father can claim prehistoric descendancy, were no longer the Jupiterian zanglodons of old,[14] but their silhouette loomed up everywhere in the antediluvian landscape.

---

[14] The zanglodon, which was never accommodated to the official jargon of biology, was a species reported to French readers by Camille Flammarion's pioneering popularization of paleontological science *Le Monde avant la création de l'homme, ou le berceau de l'univers* [The World Before the Creation of Man; or, The Cradle of the World] (1857), where it was described as a gigantic but relatively slender Triassic dinosaur. The caption of the fanciful illustration included in the text suggests that the species "might perhaps have been one of our ancestors." The original "specimen" appears to have been sold in the U.S.A. by Albert C. Koch, a showman who had exhibited a supposed sea serpent in New York in 1845 and subsequently attempted to cash in on the fashionability of dinosaur bones by faking various finds of that nature. Such was the popularity of Flammarion's work that the fictitious creature continued to enjoy a fugitive existence in the cryptozoology of Henri Coupin's oft-reprinted *Les Animaux excentriques* (1906), and a live specimen was featured in Maurice Magre's fanciful novel *Le Mystère du tigre* (1927), perhaps on a whim inspired by Dulac's novel.

They were vivipares, who drew their principle of life from the earth, of which they were the direct emanation."

"And after the Sun, what came next?"

"Venus, and then Mars, which entangled its magnetic radiations with those of the planet with the name of the goddess."

"What modifications did Venus bring to the Earth?"

"The most terrible. It caused such an upheaval in the conditions of life that the vivipares thought their last hour had come. The Sun ensured the hatching of so many eggs and the Jupiterians ate them with so much appetite that, as I've said, their strength diminished. Their faculty of procreation followed the same decadent progression. Their descendancy was proportionately smaller and precarious in its vitality. It was then that three-quarters of the animals designated by the name of prehistoric monsters disappeared. But it was also, alas, the epoch that gave birth to the first mammals. And it's here, my child, that the great secret of Brahma resides."

A long silence followed that statement. Maya held her breath, awaiting a sacred revelation, and Tussilia seemed to retreat inwardly in order to consult her spiritual Guides. When she did not speak, the child said, in a soft voice: "What is that great secret, my Lia, and who told it to you?"

"I can't—or rather, ought not to—reveal it to you until the day when amour enters into your destiny. For the moment, know that it departs from the Venusian period, and it is only since then that there have been what we now call 'males' and 'females.' That's the Truth that results from the secret that you'll know one day. The signature of Venus is on all the predatory beasts and the ruminants, on all the beings of which milk is the primary nourishment. The priests of Om also call that planet the cow Gô."

"Do I bear the seal of Venus?"

"Yes, like all women, for it's under the influence of its action that the original sin was committed. For the first time, woman—whose present form was then unforeseeable—gave birth in pain; she had emerged from an egg. That is part of the secret of Brahma, which you shall know in time."

"Are there flowers under the sign of Venus?"

"All the perfumed corollas; the others are Saturnian or Solar. The Moon has only marked the aquatic flowers."

"Why did Mars come to be mingled with the influence of Venus."

"That, no one has ever known, but the fact has remained in the memory of the first humans, who transmitted it, by way of speech, to the generations that followed. Furthermore even in our day, Mars and Venus are often in effluvial conjunction, and the earth is severely tested by it. Each of the two planets, however, has its thirty-three year cycle."

"What is the action of Mars on planets and beings?"

"It emits psychic vibrations so special that they give birth to war. Animals of the same species kill one another. Until then, the beings endowed with movement had only killed in order to eat and only ate individuals of species different from their own. From the Martian period onwards a fratricidal wrath was substituted for the rage of appetite, and the first crime was committed. Two mammals of the same form and the same blood fought over a Solar creature, and the weaker died at the hands of its brother. Amour, in its cradle—and what a cradle!—had created murder, from which so many battles were to flow. Since that accursed moment, males have risen up, without any serious motive, against other males, and males and females still oppress one another without being able to understand why. Venus and Mars are the Earth's malefic planets; they brought love and hatred to it with equal intensity."

"And after those two stars, which one emerged from the celestial vault and changed the condition of beings?"

"That was Hermes or Mercury. Have I mentioned that between each arrival of stellar forces, deluges are produced?"

"No! So there have been several of them?"

"Five. By 'deluge,' it's necessary to understand that the Being of Fire, of which we only see the cocoon, senses through the humus the new magnetism approaching it, and it shudders in its envelope, displacing the liquid in which it bathes progressively less, in a mighty swell. That's understandable, since it nourishes itself thereon, as the chicken does on the albumen of the egg, and is itself growing and undergoing transformation."

"What did your Hermes or Mercury do—to humans, for example?"

"It ameliorated their form, and then it imposed on them the unknown Host, the soul. Since then, it's the luminous and superior Host that has served the instrument that we are to manipulate the great forces of nature. Under the influence of Hermes, humans domesticated fire, ceased to nourish themselves on raw meat, and invented defensive weapons. Because of their new alimentation, they lost their rough and hairy envelope and reached, after many centuries, the biological condition that characterizes the stage of nymphs. They haven't passed that point yet, but they sense that the mutation of the incomplete animal into that of the perfect being is imminent.

"As soon as they were obliged to cover their flesh, they sensed their material inferiority, but after having vanquished the wild beast—their cousins in the original crime—they knew the ecstasy of thought. They were able to dream about the past and perceive the first glimmers of the sublime auroras of the beyond. They sensed within them, vaguely, the logic of another existence by the sensation of new energies and enlightenments. They had the revelation of Eternity, and that word enlarged the soul so greatly that it was able to measure the infinity of the Infinite.

"Since then, the Revelation by Science has served as the wireless telegraphy between humans and the divinity. Writing is Hermetic in origin. At the convent of Sakia, the oldest manuscript in the world summarizes all the science of the world before the last deluge in a single page. God is designated there by the sign of Mercury, which represents fire serving as the pedestal of the stars.[15] God is thus the attractive and cohesive force of the universe. None of the symbols adopted by each religion are worth as much as that modest hieroglyph to explain the inexplicable."

"Which are the Mercurian animals?"

"All the nymphs! To all of them, it gives the prescience of the future existence for which they are bound, and that hope furnishes the best with the courage to get through the ordeal of the final mutation."

"Which are the Hermetic plants?"

"The medicinal herbs. I forgot to add that microbes are closer to the divine principle than suns. Remember, my darling, that the impalpable is the vanquisher of matter and that the will of a gnat can extenuate the muscles of a lion. The infinitely small is the sovereign of the world."

---

[15] The astrological symbol of Mercury resembles the Venusian circle-on-a-cross, with an extra feature on top vaguely resembling a pair of horns.

"But my Lia, you talk about the impalpable as if you had seen it."

"We all see it, and every day. The frictional resin that paper attracts is an everyday example on which we don't meditate sufficiently. No one perceives the attractive force that momentarily annuls the law of gravity, but the fact is undeniable. The invisible is—and the attraction of souls to one another, sympathy and antipathy, have unknown and invisible causes. The soul is a magnetic parasite, which nourishes itself on our body."

"Could you enable me to see a soul?"

"It's quite possible, but I can more easily show you your own. Let's go home to try the experiment."

....

....

....

A great silence was established between the pupil and the Initiate. They both walked rapidly beneath the trees. The child no longer found anything to say aloud; her mind was agape, dazzled by the new light what speech had just projected into her mind. She was beginning to understand certain obscurities of her geological studies, but she trembled with fear that the veil, one corner of which had just been lifted, might conceal an illusion. At that terror, her throat contracted, her respiration became awkward, and she gazed at her grandmother avidly.

"Quickly, my Lia! I'm afraid!"

"Afraid that the mystery is being revealed?"

"Yes."

"You'll learn many others before being saturated with divine love."

....

....

....

Finally, the Villa Ourton appeared under the branches. It was eleven o'clock in the morning and the maid was out shopping. For the first time Maya saw the door of the Oratory open to her, where Tussilia spent long hours, which she took from her sleep. She thought that its walls would be decorated with precious pictures, and the room ornamented with prie-dieux sculpted like those of the chapters in cathedrals. She received a slight mental cold shower when she saw that there was nothing there but tubes of glass, retorts, bottles of all colors, and electric piles of great power.

"Close the shutters darling," said the grandmother.

When the child turned round the room was illuminated by a very soft red light.

"Sit down—and look at me, effortlessly."

Maya was scarcely breathing; she opened her pretty eyelids very wide and waited. She could not see anything—and yet, Tussilia, upright and immobile, was concentrating all her will-power.

Soon, a cry of joy emerged from the little girl's lips.

"Grandmother! Grandmother! You're giving off light! It's yellow around your head, blue around your throat and your fingers are emitting red sparks."

"That's a little of my soul. It's the theosophical aura, my darling. Each of us produces a different light. You can see mine because the red light permits the perception of the fulgurance of those magnetic emanations. Almost everyone can see luminous streaks, at least. If they escape searchers, it's because they make the mistake of trying to see them in darkness."

"And you radiate like that all the time?"

"No. When I only have calm emotions, my aura is simply gray. And now you can see yours, and make contact with the Unknown Host that you transport on earth."

"I'm scared, my Lia!"

"That's silly. Even an errant soul isn't an evil force."

So saying, the Hindu turned a commutator, and an electric crackle was audible in the silence. First, the fluid ran through a tube, and was soon captured in a sphere empty of air, but in the bottom of which a few crystals were heaped. The electricity passing over them tinted them greenish-gray; they were reminiscent of meager ashy embers on the brink of extinction

"Come closer, my darling. Approach that sphere slowly. First of all, I'll open the shutters so that the proof will be made in broad daylight. Closer! Even closer! There—do you see it?"

Maya, whose hands were seven or eight centimeters from the apparatus, saw the embers become animated, as if a new aliment were furnishing them with a stronger incandescence. The closer the child came to the sphere, the more luminous the crystals became, in spite of the glass insulating the electricity perfectly. Finally, when she touched the round surface, an intense light set the void ablaze, tinting the crystals the most vivid yellow. Flashes of emerald green and violet sparkled in the pale ocher, and the spectacle was so exciting that the girl cried: "Oh, how happy I am! That's coming from me, my Lia, my Lia!"

"Back away slowly. You see, the contact ceases and the glimmers die down; the further you draw away, the more the intensity diminishes. You can measure the present radiation of your soul. It's about seven centimeters. Look at mine."

At a distance of twenty centimeters, Tussilia's finger produced luminous phenomena in the sphere.

"I radiate further, darling, because my soul is more detached than yours. You wanted, today, to see the invisible; I've shown it to you scientifically, not by means of the trickery of a medium, whose honesty might be suspect, but by means of the intermediary of an apparatus that can't deceive.

"It's necessary to salute the name of the Comte de M , for he's the one who rediscovered, after twenty thousand years, the amometer that the ancients knew in another form. The one that served for my initiation was based on vegetal electricity—but what does the torch matter, provided that there's light? The invisible soul reveals itself by means of phenomena of luminosity—that's the essential thing.

"Now, for your first lesson of religious instruction, I've enabled you to penetrate several of the mysteries that the basis of all confessions. Kiss me, if I've been able to interest your young intelligence, and if I've given you a taste of the sacred unknown."

"Grandmother, I love you, but I'm going to love you even more. Give me, oh, give me everything that's there, inside your head. I want to know! I want to know! I sense that it's so beautiful!"

"And so simple, above all," said the grandmother, humbly.

....
....
....

Maya did not sleep at all that night, and the old Hindu was not yet awake when she went into her grandmother's bedroom.

"My Lia! My Lia! I'd like to know whether Zoar, our good dog, has a soul?"

"Yes, but not very luminous. Go look for him; you'll perceive the vague light that elementals emanate."

The fine German shepherd who protected them—especially by night—from the rare vagabonds that came through the village was brought to the laboratory and the experiment proved Madame Wiscorney correct."

"My Lia, Ghislaine told me that the soul is immortal. Is that true?"

"Yes, it's immortal in the sense that it doesn't die with the body; on the contrary, it's then that it begins its own life, exactly like every larva that abandons a victim it has devoured—but it's burned itself by the spirit that vampirizes it, before finally escaping and returning to its divine source."

"Can you enable me to see a spirit?"

"Not *a* spirit, but *the* spirit. Like the soul, it's impalpable, but our logic might be able to discern it by means of an experiment that I'll carry out before you. First, step back, because I'm going to handle the serpent that the Dalai Lama's envoy brought me when he left Lhasa to go on a mission to Ouargla. I'll be obliged, for the sake of our instruction, to make you witness a cruel spectacle. Be strong and don't move.

....
....
....

As if it were a matter of a domestic animal, Tussilia fetched a snake from a softly padded box where it was somnolent. She brought out it wound around a stick, which she then put close to a glass tube. The snake coiled around the latter gracefully, and as the magic sphere was at the end of the tube, it wound the brown spiral of its body around it.

With a prompt gesture, the old lady switched on the electricity, and Maya was able to observe that it did not produce any gleam in the crystals. The trepidation of the current, however, disturbed the animal; it raised its head and hissed loudly.

The grandmother then started singing a bizarre chant, which had something of human singing and something of birdsong in it. The animal immediately unwound its coils, retraced its path, and as soon lodged in its box.

"No trace of soul, you see...not the slightest glow...and yet, watch and meditate...

Fearlessly, without bravado, with a gesture that seemed to be familiar to her, Tussilia slid the box on to the balcony and made a sign to her granddaughter.

"My Lia, it's going to escape..."

"No it's not—it's a Houlack...which means 'a lazy one.' The species goes abroad as little as possible, and prefers fasting to hunting. But nature has been indulgent to its petty sin. Don't lose sight of it."

It was scarcely nine o'clock in the morning. The sun was bringing out birdsong and the flutter of wings in the chestnut tree that stood three meters from the house. A deafening racket of *coui-couis* and *pihouits* emerged from the emerald tent formed by the foliage. Soon, the snake tightened its coils again, thus forming a kind of pedestal, which the soil enriched with nacreous tints. Slowly, its head swayed, and then became motionless. Slightly concave at first, the reptile stiffened effortfully. The animal's eyes began to shine with a gleam that no human word can describe; it had a fixity, since its eyelids had no lashes, but it was, above all, a mute Speech.

And now, in following the trajectory of that gaze, simultaneously terrible, soft and impatient, Maya saw a little bird on a branch, which was trembling, all its feathers bristling. A lamentable, scarcely articulated chirping was emerging from its beak, which none of its brethren wanted to hear. Sparrows, chaffinches and blue tits shivered with a nameless terror and fled, on silent wings.

But an invisible force had paralyzed the locomotive nerves of the victim at a distance. What the insect had done with thrusts of its sting into the caterpillar, the snake had accomplished with its gaze alone. The state of dolorous hypnosis lasted for several minutes in the little bird, and then it seemed that it was about to escape its fate. It shook its wings, to remove it from the branch, and it succeeded in doing so. Soon, in fact, its flight striped the azure. But just at the moment when it was hastening toward salvation, the little creature made an abrupt swerve and came to perch, exhausted. There the hypnotic trance resumed—but it only lasted a few seconds. Vanquished and resigned to its destiny, the little creature fell, inertly, offering its throat, into the viscous spirals.

A little blood pearled on a wing-feather, and the snake unrolled its coils in order to savor its prey.

....
....
....

As the rites of that repast could not add anything to the demonstration that she had intended, Tussilia closed the lid of the box and took her granddaughter into the forest.

"Have you understood yet what the spirit is, my darling?"

"No. I've seen something frightful, but I'm too upset to grasp its meaning."

"I told you yesterday that the serpent was one of the first manifestations of Form. It was born of the primal clay and Saturnian forms at the time when the earth was still too hot to permit souls—magnetic beings—to nourish themselves on the monsters of that epoch. The animal in question seems to be the most disinherited of all those that move down here. It has neither arms nor legs, and yet, it's the terror of the jungle. It has nothing and it has everything, because it still holds a parcel of the Spirit of the worlds. You've seen the soul irradiate and illuminate; you've just seen the Spirit attract and kill. You can no longer doubt the three forces that rule humans as well as the universe: the body, the soul and the spirit."

"You told me that souls, when we die, go where the spirit takes them. Where does it take them?"

"Into the fluid plane, or to put it more simply, high into the air, very high up, in the confines of the terrestrial atmosphere and the Ether. Our eyes can't see them, and aviators, not understanding why they can't get through certain points, call such obstacles 'holes in the air.' Separated from our body, the soul grows and expands, then withers and cracks, and the atom of fire, devoid of light, purified, and as if distilled by the various metamorphoses it undergoes, then returns to the divine center of cohesive forces.

"The spirit precedes the body and the soul; it survives them, because it's eternal, and it never does anything other than pass into forms, fluids and matter. God has the universe for the body, light for the soul, and for the spirit the magnetic force that links the worlds. Each of us is a god in miniature. Do you understand?"

"Yes, but…I'm still very upset by the death of the bird. It came, in spite of itself, palpitating, as if dazed, to deliver itself to its killer."

"That's the entire mystery of amour!"

"Divine amour or seminal amour?"

"Both, my child."

....
....

From that day onwards, Maya paled slightly over big books and heavy manuscripts. Then it became very rare to encounter the old lady on her own among the rocks, for the girl accompanied her there fervently, and the good people of Barbizon noticed her childish gaze was taking on more of the soft and luminous expression of Tussilia's every day. Her gaiety resisted the exercises in meditation, concentration and immobility that equipped her with the gift of vision. At sixteen, she could read the thoughts of those who came near her and converse in familiar fashion with her invisible Guides, whose voices she heard as authentically as Jeanne d'Arc heard hers. A considerable number of people enjoy that auditory privilege, but few dare admit it, for fear of being accused of madness.

As the education of a Tibetan Initiate was purely scientific, and every psychic gymnastic exercise was explained methodically, it seemed quite simple to Maya that she was a kind of mage in a skirt. She had no suspicion that she was precociously evolved.

Ghislaine soon experienced a profound terror of her sister's lucidity. Two or three times she had wanted to tell her, with obligatory ornamentations, about some schoolgirl romance, and her amazement had been confined to alarm when Maya had replied: "You're mistaken, Ghislaine; that's not what happened."

"How did you know?"

"Because I can read your thoughts," the other replied, ingenuously.

The young coquette, who lied so deftly, imagined that, because the eyes are the mirror of the soul, it would be sufficient for her to lower her eyelids in order to deceive her sister's divinatory faculty, but Maya was never mistaken. It was therefore necessary to renounce triumphant repetition of the eternal refrain: "You know so-and-so? Well, he's mad about me; he wants to marry me and says he'll kill himself if I don't love him."

Maya burst out laughing every time, and put things straight.

....
....
....
....
....

Madame d'Angeville wanted to celebrate the twins' sixteenth birthday with a formal party in Paris, at her house in the Rue de Prony.

The two sisters, clad in exactly identical dresses, were equally exquisite. Ghislaine, however, knowing how to listen to gallant proposals as an impassive or enigmatic Madonna, had a great deal of success with her dancing partners.

Maya, by contrast, looked at them in such a frank and honest fashion that the gentlemen hesitated to trouble so much purity. The young ones did not know how to talk to the savage, because, in the protocol of flirtation, as soon as a phrase does not obtain the expected response, the dialogue is cut off. If fox-trotting Don Juans lose the thread of their discourse, they feel ridiculous, and never forgive. That is why any woman who does not know how to make the facets of the masculine spirit shine is quickly abandoned. The timid and the audacious were soon saying disdainfully: "She's a turkey," and, after having mocked her at a distance, condemned her to isolation.

Maya danced very little, listened a great deal and observed passionately. On her return to Barbizon, she summarized her amazement thus:

"I was very amused, Grandmother, because the young men, the young women, the old ladies and even the very old men, all seemed only to think, to talk, and to be able to talk, about amour. It seems that there's nothing interesting but that in the world. But they don't appear to know what it is! You, who make me admire every day the miracles there are in minerals, plants or animals, have enabled me to love, but the allusions that were made to me the other evening filled me with horror!"

"Didn't you meet any interesting man?"

"No...well, yes...almost. There was one very luminous aura in grandfather's house, which enveloped a handsome adolescent of twenty. You'll see him, anyway, because he's the son of Monsieur Montala, who flirts with you in the forest—you know, the one who only thinks of saving the lizards when there's a fire in the undergrowth. I told my dancing-partner that I'd introduce you to him."

"Maya...this young man pleases you..."

"Yes, my Lia, he's handsome! I'm sure that he's good. He plays tennis, likes nature, reads Schuré, Steiner and Fabre.[16] He'll please you too, I'm sure of it."

Well...look at me...uh oh! Come to the laboratory, please; I'd like to try an experiment. Carry on talking about what excited you most in Paris."

While talking about music, fabrics and perfumes, the two women went into the study room—for every day was supposed to bring its enlightenment to the mind.. Tussilia commented, by means of a lesson in physics or chemistry,

---

[16] Édouard Schuré (1841-1929) was the author of *Les Grands Initiés, esquisse d'histoire secrète des religions* (1889; tr. as *The Great Initiates; A Study of the Secret History of Religions*) and numerous other works of fiction and non-fiction treating occult matters; he was closely associated at one time with Rudolf Steiner (1861-1925), who founded his own Anthroposophical Society after breaking away from the Theosophical Society, and began an influential educational movement.

on the obscurities that had hindered the logic or meditation of her disciple.

"Come here, child, and show me your soul...or, rather, analyze its radiation."

So saying, Tussilia had put the psychic sphere in contact with the current, and magnificent gleams immediately flowed from Maya's fingers, which were touching the glass.

"Well? What do you think, my darling?"

"In truth, I recognize that I've never seen that red color before, of which there are slight patches today. It's very pretty, but what does it signify?"

"It means that before long, I shall have to transmit the secret of Brahma to you. I hope that you won't listen only to the revelation of one of the three verities that Om has hidden, thus far, from the men of the Occident. Prepare yourself for the great honor that is about to devolve upon you."

"What must I do to be worthy of it?"

"Reread Fabre, Charles Derennes, Latreille, Annie Besant, Tchoun-li-Phang and my manuscripts.[17] Then it will be sufficient for you to gaze at the forest and smile. All verity reserves for humans more tears than joy, but the truth sails for a long time over the ocean of tears, and like a skillful pilot it often saves souls in perdition."

---

[17] Charles Derennes (1882-1930) was a prolific writer of prose and poetry, particularly noted for his animal stories. Pierre André Latreille (1762-1833) was the foremost entomologist of his era, the most important predecessor of Fabre. Annie Besant (1847-1933) was one of the most prominent members of the Theosophical Society in its early years and was also famous for her campaigning for women's rights and the political independence of India (where she lived for much of her life). Tchoun-li-Phang appears to be fictitious.

"You've never spoken to me before with so much lyricism."

"That, my darling, is because you're already drawing me into the nuptial vortex of your being. From now on, I must put everything in song, for love is singing, even though one can only perceive it stammering."

"What! I'm going to love..."

"Alas, yes! To love and be loved."

....
....
....

Weeks passed.

....
....

Maya had selected for her place of meditation one of the most forbidding rocks in the vicinity of the Cheminée de Cendrillon. One morning, she suddenly shouted for help. For a quarter of an hour, Tussilia had been so detached from her corporeal housing that she was tasting the ecstasy of the blissful. That privilege of exteriorizing souls—recognized by all religions and all sciences—was the Hindu's sweetest recreation. At the cry from her grandchild, however, she reintegrated her carnal form in all haste, and, tenderly anxious, went to join the one she called, secretly, the Predestined One.

The latter was sobbing, and so much horror filled her gaze that the Initiate went pale, as she asked: "What have you seen child?"

"My Lia! My Lia! I don't want to look any more, I don't want to see—it's frightful! I saw fire, blood, mud, and everywhere the gazes of the dying, cursing their gods. They didn't want to die, and yet they were running to martyrdom. It won't happen, will it? It's too abominable! I'm afraid! I'm afraid!"

"Alas, the Martian cycle has begun, my daughter; its maleficent spiral has already bloodied the north of Asia, and will soon pass over central Europe."

"We're going to have a war, then?"

"It's necessary. The Astral Equilibrium requires it."

"Oh, Grandmother, is it possible to avoid the dramas that I've seen unfolding?"

"No, it's civilization that is forcing the nature of that hecatomb."

"Explain..."

"So long as humans hadn't surpassed the animal stage, the infinitely small were sufficient for the destruction of unnecessary or dangerous males, but as soon as iron succeeded stone and wood, as soon as the machine appeared, humans put their discoveries in the service of their antediluvian instincts. They became burrowers again, and from then on, their activity has constituted a danger for the terrestrial Being. It was therefore necessary for the planets, its parents, to ensure the safety of the future stellar nymph."

"I don't see how poor disinherited humans can trouble the planetary monster on which we live."

"Oh, my darling, don't you see, every day, robust and vigorous bodies dying, sapped, eaten away or aspired by bacilli that the microscope can barely discover?"

"That's true! Explain, my Lia, but hold my hand, because I'm still trembling at the vision I've just had."

"In brief, humans are digging down into the soil today to depths unsuspected by their ancestors, and the limit of that excavation is far from being attained. They're exploring the liquid depths with their submarines, and the air with their airplanes, and for those two elements, it's scarcely that first muttering of their future exploits. Now, neither the air, nor the sea, not the interior of the humus is destined to serve as the human domain; they're exceeding the mission that they were to fulfill in the universal economy."

"Why, then, have they been able to discover the secrets that permit them to violate nature?"

"Because the conservation of the species will necessitate, before long, the aid of the submarine and the airplane. Both will be the Arks of the sixth deluge that is in preparation. In the meantime, Mars will depopulate the world of a few million males and numerous females. Unfortunately, its sanguinary delirium will only suffice to attenuate the danger facing the planet—but it might enable it to reach the date when it will retract into its shell, bringing about a complete change in the Atlas that you know. There will be seas where there are plains today, and plains where tides agitate."

"Shall we see that?"

"No, five centuries separate us from that cataclysm. Between now and then, I hope, the Redeemer will have come, and the humans saved by submarines and airplanes will be better and more beautiful than those of our epoch."

"But if Om's envoy ameliorates humankind, there will be no more wars?"

"Obviously…but before Love can accomplish its mission of redemption. Long rivers of blood, fire and sulfur will flow."

"Prevent me from seeing the future any more, my Lia!"

"What sudden and futile cowardice, my child! All the more so as you're trembling primarily because you've seen Pierre Montala in one of your visions."

"Yes, Grandmother, I've seen him. First he was in semi-darkness in a kind of cavern, and then I discovered him afterwards in the clouds. A great lightning-bolt struck the black cross on which he seemed to be rising up to the sky, and then...I cried out! I called to you for help. He fell! He fell! Like Lucifer, like Fuschina-Li!"[18]

"Child, child...you're in love...beware of not being loved."

"Is not being loved a great misfortune, then?"

"No, but it's a real suffering."

"I'm happy, however, simply because I love..."

"It always starts like that, but afterwards...shall we go back?"

"Let's take the route via the Solitaire. I don't know why, but something draws me to that picturesque path."

"As you please. Turn right after the Lépine cross-roads."

"Oh, Grandmother, you can resume your mediation. I'll guide you safely home."

....

....

....

That day, the forest had put on its mantilla of mist. It gradually lifted as the sun rose toward the Zenith, but the moist network was still floating in the little valleys that undulated in the western reaches. The leaves glistened in the slightest sunbeam, as if they had all been freshly re-painted or varnished. The wind was shaking the crowns of the trees gently, and the moss, as well as the rocks, was receiving a double ration of dewdrops. Large quantities of tiny mushrooms had sprouted since dawn, and were already wilting in the warmth of the June sun.

---

[18] Possibly the figure from Japanese mythology more commonly known as Futsunushi, who descended to earth in some accounts, and is associated with fire, lightning and war.

Familiar with the underwood, Maya and Madame Wiscorney did not follow the blue and red markers that guided tourists in their excursions. It did not take them long to reach the Otarie, while walking between two banks of heather, already mauve, in order to reach their objective.

Having arrived at the intersection of two paths, one leading to the viewpoint at the Camp de Chailly and the other to the Chemin du Bornage, the young woman hesitated momentarily. She was trembling all over, like an insect clawed by instinct but whose antennae sense danger.

Tussilia noticed the granddaughter's agitation, without appearing to do so.

"Why am I suddenly indecisive, my Lia?" Maya asked.

"Maleficent waves must have traversed two magnets. Seek your secret desire, my child. I'll sit down here and pray, in the meantime."

"Oh, to pray for so little!"

"Destiny isn't as affected as humans, my child; it becomes tragic or comic without the slightest change of scenery. Go..."

Leaving her grandmother sitting on a tree-trunk, Maya took the path leading to Barbizon. She went at a slow pace because a sudden oppression was impeding her respiration, but her gaze searched the near horizon formed by tree-trunks standing in columns. All of her will, tormented by a vague aspiration, was causing her to listen intently. One might have thought that she was trying to catch the echo of footsteps.

Suddenly, between two oak trees, she perceived the silhouette of a man—the very one who had haunted her dreams since the evening of the ball—but a rock hid him so rapidly that she thought it was a hallucination. She hastened her pace, and, in order to distract herself—for one often shields oneself from one's own consciousness—she started humming a the tune of a children's song.

The Absorbed Rock stopped her momentarily. In the most curious mimicry of color, a tree and a rock were, in effect, contesting the place for the supremacy of the two realms of nature that they represented.

The vegetal had accepted that a mysterious law had given its bark, to a height of more than three meters from the ground, the exact blue-marbled gray tint as its neighbor, but in revenge, it had extended an enormous branch, doubtless in the crazy hope of pushing back the mineral that impeded its thrust. For decades, the branch had battled; the rock having a broad diameter at the precise point where it wanted to spread out and sway, it had broadened its base to the point of overlapping the sandstone. Then it had continued to grow, sheathing the stone. But one day, it had run short of sap, because other branches had risen up higher into the azure without caring about their elder's victory. The valiant branch had then gathered its last strength in order to form a cushion of bark, which hazard had modeled hideously into the implacable lips of a vampire.

A few meters from Maya, Pierre Montala was subject at that very moment to the emotional oppression of the sylvan tableau—but as soon as the young woman appeared, he ran toward her. They both smiled, and their hands joined, without saying a word.

Then, since it was, in fact, necessary to say something, the conventional formulae succeeded one another,

"How are you, my dear Monsieur?

"Very well, thank you. And you, how are you, Mademoiselle?"

86

"Very well, thank you."

"And..."

"Ahem..."

They both became conscious of the ridiculous banality of their dialogue. The same burst of laughter extracted them from the embarrassment.

"I wasn't expecting to encounter you," said Maya, between two joyful cascades.

"I was hoping to do so myself, for I was looking for you."

"You were looking for me? So that's it!" said the young woman, as a sudden fatigue obliged her to sit down. "Why?"

"I don't know. But it was necessary that I see you again. It was a thirst of my will—such a thirst that it seemed to me that you were calling to me."

"Oh!" Maya groaned, as if someone had snatched away the last of her veils.

"It's a pity that it isn't true, because I found such great sweetness in the thought."

"Why?"

"Because... I don't know!"

For that question and the response both young people had raised their eyes simultaneously, and each one was searching the other's eyes for the key to the enigma that was troubling them.

Fortunately, youth has the privilege of ecstasy, before sinking into the contingencies of matter, so the young people were not in any state to analyze their sensations, any more than to philosophize about their situation. They were subject to the tender double law that regulates souls and the flesh.

As they had not found the response either to their "Why?" or their "Because," in the ingenuous flash of the gaze that they had exchanged, a silence fell upon their joy. But a man of twenty does not persevere for long in the search for the solution to a difficult problem. Unable to do anything better, Pierre Montala reported:

"I'm happy," he said. "I'm happy, I'm happy...I breathe more easily by your side; the light is more vivid, the forest more vibrant. Listen to the rustling of the trees. Is it necessary to be stupid to run around the woods, when there's so much good in solitude...?"

"You're forgetting my presence!"

"Me? Oh no—but it seems to me that you've melted into me, amalgamated with me, and that I'll be alone henceforth everywhere that you are not."

"Stop! Stop! That's a declaration! Oh, don't worry, the savage that I am knows that it's a long way from the rim of the well to...the Truth."

"I swear to you that my thoughts are lovelier, more ardent and more sincere than the words of the poor human language could ever be. Since I first saw you, I feel that I've been captured body and soul by your smile. I have the impression that a divinity resides in you, and that I'm coming, as a faithful believer, to bow down before you."

"The pleasure with which I listen to you, my dear Monsieur, causes me a vague intimate terror—so I invite you to come with me. I'll introduce you to my grandmother."

"Not yet! It's so pleasant like this. Remain sitting down, I beg you, and let's not say anything. Listen to my heart; it's beating fast enough to make my chest burst."

"Why?"

"A man never knows the profound causes of something that makes him tremble, laugh or weep. I feel happy, and that verity is singing within me like a hosanna, like a *Te Deum*. As I repeat those words, it seems to me that you're saying 'Thank you!' Because it's from you, from your presence, that I'm obtaining this whirlpool of joy that is giving me vertigo. You're the source of a bliss so new for me that I don't know what name to give it."

"It's doubtless amity."

"Yes…perhaps…but I'm sure of never having been troubled so deliciously."

Maya, who was beginning to be paralyzed by those tender words, had a surge of wisdom. She got up abruptly and drawing two paces away, insisted: "Let's go find my Lia."

With one bound however, Pierre Montala had stood up, and, retaining her gently, protested passionately: "No, please, a moment more!"

"Oh!" moaned the young woman.

"Did I hurt you?"

"No… it's an image that suddenly surged forth in response to your gesture. It seemed to me that you were a cat playing with a mouse…"

"But I'm not thinking about eating you. My dream is solely to kiss your hand."

So saying, Pierre Montala raised Maya's fingers to her lips, lingered in the hollow of four dimples, and was certainly about to reach the satined amber of the wrist when Madame Wiscorney's voice put a stop to his audacity.

"If gazes are the kisses of souls, human kisses are the vampires of souls, Monsieur."

Confused, the young man blushed and bowed to the Initiate.

"Grandmother, I introduce to you one of my dancing partners. He's the son of the greatest friend of the forest, after you—that's enough to say that it's a matter of Monsieur Montala."

While chatting, Tussilia, her smile indulgent and her hand welcoming, examined the aura displayed to her. Pierre, in any case, rendered that study facile, for, dazzled by the Initiate's luminous gaze, he was subject to its irresistible charm...and, after a few minutes of conversation, he had surrendered all his secrets.

"I hear," she concluded, as a charming grandmother, "that you'll be glad to offer me your homage, in order to in order to increase your chances of applying for promotion to the rank of Maya's dancing partner for the impending winter."

"That's it exactly, but perhaps not all," said Pierre, with the laugh of an intimated scamp.

"It's enough for today, though," Tussilia replied, more gravely. "Let's see, now, what auguries I ought to take from the place where our meeting has taken place...Aie! I don't much like that!"

"What is it, my Lia?"

"That symbol of the struggle of the realms of nature, that tree and that rock...and then...this..."

With her index finger, the Hindu pointed to the most impressive design that the rain, the sun and the winds has ever traced on a rock.

"Oh!" said Pierre. "How curious that is! One might think that it's a Venetian mask, letting the gaze of two tender and anguished eyes filter through."

"I've never noticed it!" said Maya. "Indeed, the more one looks at the triangle, the more one discerns the arch of the eyebrows, the globe of the eye, the birth of the nose...and then...but it gives me gooseflesh...positively, one might think it the gaze of a martyr condemned to a feudal *in pace*."

"Alas, it's more tragic still."

"Brrr! That sculpture of hazard is hallucinatory! Don't you think so, Madame?"

"Yes, yes—let's go! Go on ahead, my children."

While the young people headed for the main road, Tussilia remained for a few seconds, with her arms folded before the stone mask. She stared at it harshly, like a dominatrix whom fear cannot trouble; then, slowly, she aimed her two index fingers at the two strange eyes. A magnetic spark sprang forth a few centimeters from the rock, and the Initiate, increasingly arrogant and uptight, murmured:

"That man is really the Predestined, then, since you wanted to see him? You shall not kill him; I take him under my protection, for from him or his descendants, the Redeemer will be born. He's marked for the astral, as you are for the material. Your rage will be impotent. I've understood…it's war! And I'm on guard! Let Saturn not devour too quickly, in you, its last and most terrible child."

Having moistened her right thumb with saliva, she made the sign of Om on the stone and drew away, grave and hieratic.

....
....
....
....
....

While autumn covered the moving dome of the forest with rust, gold and copper, hunting and tennis served as pretext for Montala's son to visit Barbizon, every week from Saturday to Monday.

His father, indulgent for what he believed to be a simple crush, said to his wife: "Let him go—he's infatuated, I tell you. One doesn't fight against sixteen-year-old sorceresses." He was, however, slightly anxious about the ascendancy that the Wiscorney ladies were obtaining over his son. The latter sometimes returned to Barbizon with his head heavy with ideas that his worthy father did not understand at all.

Several times, the father had even dined at the Villa Ourston, and he had always come back with his logic overturned but his spirit appeased. He took an extreme pleasure in listening to Madame Wiscorney, and loved to find himself in the radiation of her large exotic eyes. Furthermore, the cuisine was excellent, and Maya seemed the most banal ingénue in the world. He did not, therefore, think that he ought to raise any obstacle to an amiable and pure idyll.

Such was his opinion when, after a hunting-party at Barbizon on the twenty-first of December 1913, he attempted, between two pipes, to convince his friend Robert Dunant that the Hindu was not merely an eccentric.

The boar-hunter was determinedly hostile to the occult sciences, but he knew the celebrated observation by Cuvier: "For a long time, chemistry passed for an occult science," and he understood very well that only the ignorant gave the term the mysterious sense that clung to it like a clothes-moth. He preferred to deny completely, however anything that surpassed his acquired knowledge, so all that he retained from his comrade's confidences was an enigmatic datum: "There's a Tibetan priestess in Barbizon and a Crazy Rock in the forest. Which of them is making mock of the world?"

He allowed himself to be introduced to the two grandmothers and the two twins, and, as dusk falls rather abruptly in the countryside in winter, Madame d'Angeville and Ghislaine, having to go home that evening, accepted Louis Dubar's offer to accompany them back to Paris.

Traveling was already very difficult before the war for two women of the world who had a horror of crowds and jostling. During the journey, the young advocate was able to gain the sympathy of Madame d'Angeville, and conceived a foolish pride in having made Ghislaine blush two or three times. He had, however, only gazed at her with a slight persistence.

Another one! thought the Don Juan in leggings. *The aurora of love reflects its ruby-colored clouds over the cheeks of conquered virgins. There's a Madonna who'll give me a nice cathedral flirtation.*

And with his right hand he sharpened the tip of the moustache that he wore. in the French style, like all the men of that epoch.

....

....

While the other hunters went back to Paris in a smoking compartment, playing poker in a veritable fog poisoned by nicotine and the reek of kennels, Pierre Montala and his father were playing bridge at Madame Wiscorney's house. The night was already well-advanced when they went back to their hotel. Once in his room, Pierre was not a little surprised to find a sealed envelope on his pillow bearing no subscription but his initials. He tore open the flap and read:

Before the return of the moon, and under the gaze of the Immured, take the road to the Solitaire, and go past the Great Corpse guarded by eleven lances. You will find yourself then in the grotto of the Otarie. Search with your eyes for the Crazy Rock. When you have seen it change location three times, in spite of the fear that will grip you, speak to it; it will reply.

"What does that mean? Pierre could not help saying, and thought:

It's a joke in bad taste. The Crazy Rock is taking me for a fool! Naturally, I won't go to the pretended rendez- vous; I've no desire to be the laughing-stock of the neigh- borhood. And what's the Immured anyway? What gaze? What Corpse? What genie is taking me for an idiot?

"Overcome the fear that will grip you!" Fear, me! In fact, everyone here is afraid of the Crazy Rock. It must be a joke of my dear Papa's. Oh well...tomorrow, instead of leaving by the nine o'clock train I'll take the eleven o'clock and I'll send him back this note:

Papa. I'll give your compliments to the Immured and kiss the Crazy Rock. You're quite a joker! Your respectful son, Pierre.

....

....

Having written those words, the young man went to bed, but it was impossible for him to sleep. In brief night- mares, he saw Maya buried under masses of rocks, or he went astray in a prehistoric chaos from which a voice emerged from every stone calling for help. He woke up several times in the grip of a frightful terror, and ended up getting up at first light, with the intention of going to soothe his nerves by means of a long walk.

However, he did not neglect to slide the note, which he thought very witty, under his father's door. He did not suspect that Monsieur Montala would go pale on reading it, and exclaim fearfully: "Is my son going mad? I believe that it's high time to get him away from Hindu priestess- es."

....

....

A chilly mist blurred the skeletons of the forest trees, and beneath the gleam of the pale dawn, one might have thought that every beech or fir had donned a diaphanous gray nightgown in order to sleep. The wind could gallop along the avenues, writhe and whistle over their heads, but they slaked the thirst of their dream with the cold dew, of which the shriveled dead leaves on the ground retained a few drops in their maroon shroud.

All the shutters were closed in the village, and Pierre headed mechanically for the part of the Bornage where the walls of the Villa Ourton rose up. He walked slowly through the mist, receiving on his shoulders all that the denuded branches could shake off, of water, twigs and russet leaves. A singular frisson made the branches tremble, and a common dolor was exhaled in the creaking of two twin trees. The silhouette of a fleeting animal traversed the undergrowth. It made off, carrying a dying prey in its jaws.

And then there was silence—an agonizing silence that stopped the young man's stroll dead, so strongly did he experience the sensation of invisible beings falling silent in order to be better able to attack him. Fear is often merely the vague perception of forces whose contours sights cannot make out clearly, but whose maleficent power to the soul dreads. A sudden serenity invaded him, however. He had just recognized, two meters away, the shutters of the room where Maya was doubtless sleeping the slumber of vestals.

The mist blurred the outline of the villa. Moist phantoms floated along the walls, and the cerebral effervescence that amour imprints on the human brain had soon launched the handsome adolescent into the most ardent and the most romantic dream. The enamored turned to melancholy, however, when a slender brown form hieratically enveloped in a kind of hooded cape crossed the road without even looking at him. Entirely given over to his meditation, Pierre continued to cultivate delirium in his thoughts.

Suddenly, a sort of irritation imposed itself on his nerves, and his will was abruptly divided between the desire to prolong his dream and the imperious need to go away. Where? He did not know—but it was necessary for him to walk: to march! As if he had been caught by an invisible thread drawn by an irresistible force, he tore himself away from the Chemin du Bornage and abandoned himself to the strange ambulatory mania that possessed him.

Without knowing why, he took the Chemin des Mazettes, turned abruptly to his left, passed in front of the Grand Majoré and felt quite disorientated when he arrived on the main road. He was anxious, nervous and in a bad mood, like a dog vexed at having lost the trail it was following.

A path opened in front of him on the other side of the great macadam artery, but it seemed to him that a silhouette was profiled there in the mist, so he took a path almost parallel to that one, and plunged into the forest aimlessly. After a short while, however, no longer perceiving any stroller, he could not hold back an irrational desire to rejoin the path that he had voluntarily avoided. And he was overjoyed when, after a few strides, he found himself directly in front of the Absorbed Rock.

Paying no heed to the cold and damp, he sat down, and rediscovered, by way of the magic of memory, the sweet emotion of his encounter with Maya.

I was here…she arrived that way…and…

Suddenly, the charming image that he had evoked vanished, and a great chill penetrated his heart. His gaze had fallen, by chance, on the famous stone mask, whose tragic eyes seemed to be staring at him intensely.

He shivered, and sensed that he had gone pale. Boldly, however, he got up, his arms folded, in order better to defy the troubling radiation that the play of the light was causing to spring from the rock.

Then, as no threat responded to his heroic pose, he thought that he was being ridiculous, and smiled. He even thought that the strange gaze had a very benevolent expression.

Pierre sat down again, silently.

The man and the stone exchanged vibrations. The mask seemed to say to the adolescent: "I'm sad and you're going to be happy! You're free and I'm a prisoner!"

And all of a sudden, the adolescent remembered the note that he had found on his pillow the night before: *under the gaze of the Immured, take the road to the Solitaire...*

But in that case, he thought, without being able to analyze his impressions, *it can't be a joke of Papa's...*

He sensed, at that moment, that he was the victim of dominant wills. And as no instinct rebelled within him, a joyful intoxication invaded him. He had acquired, by his reading, so-called magical verities, and he was enchanted, delighted, to be living a psychic adventure of his own. Without further delay, he decided to hasten to his rendezvous with the Crazy Rock.

He scanned the enigmatic written invitation several times...and...first saluting the cold gaze that was haunting him with a smile, he strode over the ground in a rigorous straight line. He reached a distinctly-traced path, but did not know whether to turn left or right, when a little sign with a faded inscription attracted his attention. Slowly, he deciphered: *Chemin du Solitaire*—and his entire body trembled with a joyous frisson. Without intending to, he had accomplished the first stage of the strange rendez-vous. Now, he had to go on to the end of the adventure.

"Now for the Great Corpse guarded by eleven lances!" he said aloud, laughing.

A sudden gust of wind carried his hat away, and in order to pick it up he was obliged to plunge eastwards into the forest. Eddies in the air carried the hat away several times just as he was about to reach it, and he became slightly hesitant. He turned around several times and suddenly stood still, his heart a trifle unsteady.

He had just perceived, to his right, one of those giant oaks struck by lightning decades ago, which remained upright, by virtue of one of those prodigies that defy the laws of nature. Its trunk and branches, completely hollowed out, ought to have collapsed at the first gust of wind, and yet, the squalls of numerous winters had respected its skeleton.

As if to render it posthumous honors, eleven junipers, growing like lances, surrounded the misery of its soft bark.

"That's obviously the Great Corpse in question…but…of whom or what am I the plaything? Let's go on to the grotto of the Otarie all the same. I'll have the key to the enigma!"

He would have liked, however, not to be alone. So, when, after walking some distance at random—he believed—he perceived a brown silhouette in the distance, he did not hesitate to call out to the unknown individual. But the mist sent back to him the echo of his own voice; it seemed to him to be toneless and quavering with emotion. Then he stiffened himself in order not to cry out, and like a somnambulist he went on, his arms groping the empty air, straight ahead.

Weary, with a lassitude he had never experienced before, he soon wanted to rest, and when he saw the opening of the grotto before which a vague sandstone sea-lion mounted guard, he murmured: "Finally, I can sit down!"

In the penumbra of the narrow cavern, he let himself fall on to a stone, and sponged his face while inspecting the rocks in the vicinity.

The silence of that corner of the forest is very impressive, even in ardent sunlight. In the heavy atmosphere of that December morning, however, there was something sinister about it. Gray and icy vapors were crawling, breaking up and shifting like languid phantoms.

After a few moments, Pierre Montala, fearful, joked in order to give himself courage. "The Crazy Rock is late!" he said, making a megaphone of his hands.

With a sound of rustling silk, however, a heavy triangular mass installed itself on the nearby summit of an enormous boulder. There it remained, motionless.

A cold sweat beaded the young man's temples. Nevertheless, without hesitation, he ran forward to cross the five or six meters that separated him from the mysterious Rock. He had not got half way, though, when the rock had disappeared.

The phenomenon was reproduced three times in less than ten minutes, and Pierre, vexed at being mocked, even by a genie, was impelled to a foolish anger. With invective on his lips and his fist clenched, he howled: "I don't believe in magic—I'm not an imbecile! And the practical joker who's making fun of me will soon receive the only thing he merits."

But a soft voice close to him whispered, as if in his ear: "Come to find me at the Cheminée de Cendrillon. I'm not afraid..."

"Me neither!" exclaimed the young man.

And without further delay, he set about rushing down a rocky path, in order to get to the rock, which hazard had carved into the form of a rustic hearth, more rapidly. But he went astray for a few minutes, and when he arrived at the rendezvous his amazement was immense to find Madame Wiscorney sitting there, tranquil and grave. She was not wearing any kind of hood and her silhouette of an old aristocratic lady did not remind Pierre in any way of the brown outline of the stroller in the mist.

"It's good to be punctual, my friend," said the Hindu, smiling, extending her hand.

"You haven't asked me so far as I know, to come here! Do you imagine that a practical jo...?"

"Shh!" I know!"

"What! The Crazy Rock—that was you?"

"No, but I know its secret."

"This trick seems to me to be unworthy of you, Madame," Pierre growled.

"Never, on the contrary, have I been more serious— and you'll bless me shortly, if you'd care to come back to Barbizon with me..."

"Only too happy...certainly...," he said, overcoming his anger, like a well brought-up person.

"Monsieur," said Tussilia, "I brought you here to ask you a very important question."

"Couldn't you formulate it at your house instead of rendering me ridiculous?"

"No, because it was necessary for me to test your telepathic sensitivity and exercise the power of human magnetism on your nerves in order to engage in this dialogue."

"Oh, Madame, the science of Mages doesn't attract me at all—and I won't be so grotesque another time!"

"Male pride having uttered its protest, in an anticipated challenge, I'll continue. Young man, you please me greatly, which doesn't matter to you, but you also please Maya infinitely. Then again, I wanted to know what the significance is, for the future, of your assiduous visits and the joyful sympathy that you manifest for my granddaughter."

"Oh, I haven't the slightest hesitation in answering you. I love Mademoiselle Maya, I love her recklessly. The air she doesn't breathe oppresses me. Barbizon can compare, so far as I'm concerned, with the terrestrial Paradise. My heart beats in her smile and my thoughts express themselves by means of her lips. My father says that I'm an idiot, that it will pass and that he knows better than I do what I call love."

"Oh, neither he nor you have the slightest notion of it; you don't even suspect your ignorance," the calm Tussilia remarked, serenely.

"You think so? You think that my father and I don't know..."

"Anything about love, I repeat. Now, as I have to reveal the great mystery to you, if you are the one promised to Maya by Destiny, it's necessary that you affirm your situation as fiancé at the Villa Ourton very soon. The divulging of the secret of Brahma ought to be surrounded by all possible security, and I'll expect Monsieur Montala's official request before receiving you."

"I hope, Madame, to convince my parents to fulfill that requirement of protocol very soon—but what is this secret of Brahma that you seem to be making the pivot of my happiness?"

"The great Truth, Monsieur! If, having received it, you understand it, and make it the spiritual bond of your union with Maya, I shall be able to retire to the mountain and dissolve myself in Om, to the right hand of Kacyapa."

"Excuse me, Madame, if I don't speak the same religious language as you, but I retain from this conversation that Maya loves me, that I adore her, and that if Papa asks you, you'll give her to me. My happiness is immense, my head is reeling, I have a desire to kiss y…the trees, the pebbles…and, if you permit, the end of your scarf too."

"Good, good…chatter away, young romantic—but remember this, which is absolutely necessary: if you want to come to my house again you must obtain the formal consent of your parents. You must reread the work of Fabre, especially the chapter on the *Anthrax* and its larva.[19] You must meditate on Steiner's Initiation, and read the books I shall send you—for you'll only return to the Villa Ourton if you agree to that, and consent to receive the three Sacred Lessons. Finally, I'll ask you for your word of honor that, between now and then, you won't try to see Maya again; that you won't write to her, and that you won't have any verbal message communicated to her. She's aware of the step I'm taking in your regard, and will spend the ten days that I'm fixing as an interval in psychic meditation. If, by chance, her ardent will leads her, by means of a phenomenon of ubiquity, to show herself to you, be prudent, and don't try to approach her—you'd do her great harm. I'm waiting for your word."

"I give it to you, Madame. I incline before your desires. I'll go away without seeing your granddaughter again—but I don't understand what your allusion to Mademoiselle Maya's gift of ubiquity signifies."

---

[19] The larvae of flies of the *Anthrax* genus parasitize other insects, most notably bees. The rather gruesome life-cycle in question is described in detail in a chapter in Fabre's *Souvenirs entomologiques* translated into English in the popular digest *Fabre's Book of Insects*.

"It signifies that my daughter can appear, material but impalpable, some distance from the place where her body is entranced."

"I don't really understand, but I won't insist."

"That is, however, part of the science of Brahma. The Peuhls,[20] The Caledonians of the forest and a few Mongols practice that magnetic disengagement fairly fluently. But here we are back at the Bornage. Return to Paris, but before then, look at me, search my thought! You sense that I'm entirely on your side, don't you? Then...be brave...Kacyapa is watching over you!"

....
....
....

The days that followed brought young Montala nothing but chagrin and disillusionment. First of all, his father, mother and aunt competed in indignation. Then, after a sort of family council, the consent was unanimously refused. Madame Montala, in order to weaken her son's will, had recourse to the science of tears and despair. Finally, his friends tried to kill Maya's prestige by means of ridicule.

"She's as mad as her grandmother," said one.

"She's a snake-charmer, a witch, offer her a toad and a screech-owl," said another.

And enormous and strident laughter further aggravated the martyrdom that those words inflicted upon the worthy fellow.

Nevertheless, he conscientiously reread the ten volumes of Fabre, and involuntarily, new enlightenment was born in his mind. In order to forget the sarcasm of fools,

---

[20] "Peuhl" is one of the French versions of the name of the African people usually known in English as the Fula or Fulani.

he tried to absorb the exercise of will prescribed by Steiner, and it seemed to him that a new sense was born within him.

Finally, on the seventh day of his Calvary, the postman brought a manuscript, the reading of which plunged him into such delight that he dared, the following day, to approach his father again.

The latter was so violent, so categorical and so abrupt that Pierre fled the family home, his eyes haggard and his gestures crazy. He ran straight ahead, without paying any heed to obstacles, without hearing the curses of the people he bumped into.

He suddenly found himself calm and lucid in the Église de la Trinité. Fatigue caused him to collapse on a chair, and the charm of the religious silence completed the relaxation of his nerves. After a few minutes, he wept desperately, discouraged. He truly did not know what he ought to do, and he rebelled against being so unjustly tortured by the people he loved most on earth.

"What can I do? My God, what can I do?" he said, in spite of himself, between two sobs.

And, raising his eyes to the altar two meters away, he saw...coming toward him...Maya! Yes Maya, diaphanous and yet normal in color and form. He was about to launch himself toward her when Tussilia's instruction came back to mind.

Don't try to approach her...

It was true, then. The woman he loved was one of those privileged individuals who could renew the prodigies of Indians, Lamaists and Saints. Involuntarily, with his hands joined and his eyes misted, he repeated: "What can I do? My God, what can I do?"

It seemed to him, although he did not hear any sound, that Maya had replied to him: "It's necessary to love me, since I love you."

He shivered in fear and in joy when the young woman brushed his forehead and his lips with her fingertip. Then he no longer saw anything around him, and he breathed deeply.

As if by magic, all sadness and all anguish had flown away from his heart. A great appeasement flowed through him, like a delightful freshness. And without debating with his conscience for an instant, he knew what he had to do.

"I shall marry Maya," he declared, positively. "But how, in three days, can I overcome my parents' resistance?"

....
....
....

When Pierre returned home at seven o'clock, his mother welcomed him with a great cry: "Finally, there you are! How frightened I was, after this morning's scene! I beg you, don't persist in trying to impose that granddaughter of Satan on us—for Madame Wiscorney is certainly a demon."

"Come on, Maman..."

"The proof is that after your departure this morning, your father, still furious over your resistance, went into his study. How amazed he was to see the old lady, whom I don't know, sitting at his desk and tranquilly writing on a piece of blank paper.

"'Oh, damn it!' he shouted. 'If you like we can finish with this business of an engagement right away!' Quite undisturbed, the lady looked at your father in a fashion that was both troubling and imperious. Then, without a gesture, *pfft!* She disappeared. How? Where? I don't understand it at all. The door was closed and the window too. But your father isn't mad, since I saw the word she had written in a beautiful elongated cursive."

"What word?"

"*Come!* Without any other form of politeness. And just like that—he went!"

"To Barbizon?"

"Yes. His rage was such that I fear, for Madame Wiscorney, the outburst of a rather brutal anger. Your father's vocabulary is sometimes a trifle rude. I'm dying of anxiety. He'll doubtless come back this evening, by train..."

Footsteps were heard at that moment, and then the drawing room door opened. Monsieur Montala came in. His wife and son dared not say a word.

"Well, be satisfied, Pierre," said the new arrival. "I've promised my consent to your marriage, and I took a cab in order to bring you the news more rapidly."

"With the witch?" cried the mother.

"Mother! Mother!"

"I refuse mine! I haven't raised my son to be the prey of Hell!"

"Don't say such stupid things, will you! Hell...Hell...anyway, your consent is purely formal; mine is sufficient."

"Papa! Papa! Thank you, thank you!" said Pierre, transported. "By what miracle have you changed your mind?"

"Don't ask me—I don't know. I don't know anything. I arrived at the Villa Ourton with insults on my lips, but I couldn't formulate any of my arguments. I found Maya in tears and Madame Wiscorney smiling. A quarter of an hour later I declared myself vanquished and Maya embraced me wholeheartedly. I'm curbed, broken! I need to sleep. Leave me alone. Have dinner without me."

....

....

....

The meal that followed that vague explanation was punctuated by long silences and vehement exclamations. Madame Montala took Heaven as her witness for what she called the "bewitchment" of her two men. She talked in the most serious fashion possible about having them exorcised. And the fear of Satan's maledictions haunted the poor devotee's mind to such an extent that she did not hear any of Pierre's protests and supplications.

War-weary, the young man quit the table, picked up his hat and went out into the scintillating darkness of the Paris night. He went straight ahead, his soul glad and all of his youth so exultant that he smiled at all the powdered strollers who promised him exceptional delights. He did not stop for any of them, but he did not cease smiling, talking to himself in a whisper.

He was so radiant with joy that one prostitute— already on the turn, having become philosophical by dint of humiliations received—walked alongside him for a few moments without him noticing the fact.

"Hey, handsome lad," she said, finally, "what's her name, today's joy?"

"Maya," he could not help replying. "Maya! Maya! If you knew…"

"Shh! Shut up, child, shut up! Misfortune's on the prowl, hide your secret."

For a moment, Pierre contemplated the benevolent eyes, like those of a beaten dog, which the fast life had wrinkled with creases and swellings. Then his gaze descended to the weary and faded mouth, of which Wisdom had just made use to impede the profanation of his love, and something akin to tenderness softened his thoughts.

"You're a good girl," he said. "Look, go home—here's two louis."

"That's nice! One last piece of advice, then, if you like. You go home too, kid. The Parisian night soils pure dreams. You're not the first I've protected from his own nerves. Go home, I tell you. Right away!"

In order to convince him, the hoarse voice of the whore recovered such a maternal tenderness, and such an urgency, that he hailed a taxi.

....
....
....

At the Villa Ourton Maya had been singing since dawn. Her being was bathed by such joy that she allowed herself to follow the thread of her destiny without the slightest apprehension. However, when Tussilia had left her, she had noticed the excessive pallor of her grandmother's face

"Are you in pain, my Lia?"

"No, but I have to give you the first Sacred Lesson today and I can't help feeling a great emotion. I'm going to prepare myself with prayer and immobility. Give Pierre lunch when he arrives, for he doesn't have the habit of fasting, as we do. Only take an infusion of marjoram, and bring your fiancé to the Chaos of Yama."[21]

"You're leaving me alone when he's coming? I might faint with joy, and you won't be there?"

"Go on, child—although certain moments were refused to my youth, I now that they ought to be savored in

---

[21] Yama is the Hindu god of death, having been promoted to that position after being the first mortal to die.

private, without a witness. I have faith in your goodness, and in any case, my Genii are protecting you. Until later."

When the Initiate was no more than a brown dot in the paths of the forest, Maya ran to her mirror. The glass informed her that her hair was not seductive enough; she tried several styles. Then she slipped into a supple white dress and, for the first time, perceived how the open air had unfortunately tanned her beautiful arms. There were also a few freckles on her cheeks.

"He'll think I'm ugly! May God, what can I do? What can I do?"

Her meager powder puff spent a bad quarter of an hour. Finally, the mirror deigned to find that the fiancée's ensemble might satisfy a difficult gallant. Then Maya thought about making a few sandwiches and a pot of coffee.

As always happens in such cases, the interested party arrived before the table was laid.

Pierre and Maya suddenly found themselves in confrontation, mute, awkward and delighted. She held out her hands and, after taking them, he drew her to his heart. He did not even think about kissing her. He put his arms around her gently, and chastely.

"Mine! Mine! You're mine, aren't you?" said the radiant young man.

"Not yet," joked the young woman. "Your proprietorial instinct is betraying your thought."

But he pressed her more tenderly to his breast. A silence followed that age-old gesture. Then, as no words could express the nuptial vertigo that set their ears abuzz like a swarm of bees, they looked at one another ecstatically.

"I love you," Pierre murmured. "Oh, how I love you."

"Again…say it again: *I love you!*"

"Yes, but you…do you love me?"

"Idiot! Who doesn't perceive that I've replied to you. Say those three words again: *I love you!*"

"Oh, this time the tone's more accurate, I understood! But you're a little hypocrite!"

"It's not hypocrisy, it's modesty. And since you don't understand the language of young women at all, hurry up and have lunch, because grandmother's waiting for us in the forest, for the hymeneal initiation of Brahma."

"A strange woman, Madame Wiscorney, my darling! Only last week I considered her…respectfully, but still…a little bit eccentric. Today, I'm torn between a desire to learn all the great secrets from her and a vague terror of being drawn into troubling errors."

"It's necessary not to doubt, Pierre, since I believe."

"And then, what does it matter? Your faith will be mine; and if a mirage is deceiving your reason, I want to share the illusion that is dear to you…I love you, Maya!"

....
....
....

Tussilia had scarcely recovered from the inevitable exhaustion that follows a deep trance when she looked at her watch.

"Noon!" she said, smiling. "Ah, youth, youth!"

Her legs still unsteady, she got to her feet. Drops of sweat were pearling on her forehead; her cheeks retained, in two damp furrows, the tracks of the last tears that the supreme and last psychic appeal had extracted from her. Having restored the serenity of her features and resumed her customary expression of mild gravity, she stood on a rock and surveyed the forest with her eyes.

A charming smile immediately extended the pure arc of her mouth, for she had perceived Pierre and Maya in the distance, lost in their dream, and heading as slowly as possible for the assigned rendezvous. The slightest briar caused the young man to leap forward as an urgent protector; he moved the plant aside to enable the young woman to pass by, as if he had saved her from the greatest peril.

But that role soon displeased Maya; she escaped, running to the right, hiding the left, and plunging straight ahead—in brief, without thinking any longer about her grandmother, both of them started playing something akin to a game of tag, punctuated with mad laughter and strident squeals.

But Tussilia called out to them.

Then, slightly confused, the young couple came to join her, and Pierre was very intimidated by the greeting she addressed to him.

"Blessed be the envoy of God! May the earth be propitious to him and may the Redeemer choose him among all," said Madame Wiscorney.

With the same ease that she would have had in the most welcoming of drawing rooms, the old Hindu offered the young couple two low-set stones to sit on.

"Not very soft, the pews of the Temple," Pierre joked.

"I agree," said Tussilia, "but at least you'll be sheltered from the sun while I instruct you."

"Don't you fear the ardor of the midday sun, Madame?"

"On the contrary, it's necessary to me. We're assured of solitude, as you can see, for no path is nearby, and it's the hour when people avoid the sun's rays. No human being but you, my dear predestined ones, should hear the sacred revelations. You have the right to ask me questions, but I ask you only to do so during my pauses; don't trouble my trances, nor my ecstasies."

On hearing those words, Pierre could not help thinking that, all the same, the old lady was a trifle bizarre, but he rectified that thought himself. Did not the lives of the Saints, of which he had read many, speak, in sum, of ecstasies and exceptional physical states? Were the Saints not merely human beings endowed with ultra-sensitive nerves? Why should the phenomena that rendered them piously humble not by reproduced, in spite of the different interpretation that might be given to them?

Grave and respectful, he waited, but his deference could not resist the need that he felt to hold Maya's hand in his.

Tussilia, standing on a rock, her arms extended as if for a benediction, evoked the image of ancient priestesses. The expression of her eyes no longer had the luminous gleam whose seduction was inescapable. She was no longer looking ahead but within, and in the impressive silence of that frame, which evoked the universal chaos of which Mythology, the Bible, the Koran and all holy books evoke, she intoned a kind of chant. Her slightly hoarse voice rose up nevertheless very softly and very captivating, while the sunlight, falling vertically upon her head, set flames in her hair, illuminated her flesh and rimmed the whole of her brown silhouette with an impalpable golden halo.

. . . .
. . . .
. . . .

The First Lesson of Brahma

"O you, young friends, whom the heavens have designated for the realization of the great mystery, O you whom love has magnetized toward one another, learn the truth of amour. It annuls all theories with which men instruct one another, overturns all the laws of biology, explains all the mysteries of the heart and the spirit. It is the Truth, the only Truth, the true Truth! Since you are to be united by the bonds that humans have made official, learn the history of your carnal genesis, then that of the parasite that is the immediate connection linking matter to the impalpable. You will then know the mission that is devolved to you.

"And first, the Capital Verity:

"*In this world, there are neither males nor females.*

"There are only females, some of them vivipares and others ovipares.

"The creatures that are called, improperly, 'males' are the criminal survivors of antediluvian species. They are only parasites.

"You know, both of you, since you have read my manuscripts, what modifications Jupiter, the Moon and the Sun imposed upon beings issued from the fermentation of the elements, I need only speak to you today about the genesis of humanity.

"As soon as the ovipares appeared, the monsters greedy for molten metals were their bitter enemies. The formidable vertebrates with enormous bones, whose strength sowed fear beneath the humid and low skies of that epoch, savored the vegetables and eggs that the sun was to cause to hatch.

113

"The evaporation of the water that maintained the minerals in the state of alimentary mud was the cataclysm by which the giant races were overwhelmed. The most solid jaws and the most robust stomachs could not vanquish the solidification of matter. Only the smallest Jupiterians survived, because the law of evolution always strikes the strongest.

"Among those which survived the desiccation of their nourishment there was one rather hideous being that the sacred designs represent with the body of a toad, the head of a horse and a tail in the form of a pickax, on which it leaned in order to stand upright. That tail was both a redoubtable weapon and a tool; it served ordinarily for heaping up the earth after having dug it out, in order to oppose a resistance to perpetually unleashed elements. It was to that extremely ugly animal, to be sure, that the Sacred Science traces back the human race. Like its contemporaries, it had neither fur not a mane, since the first fleeces only date from the cycle of Venus.

"More intelligent that the monsters with formidable jaws, the Kastéhus—that was the name of the human ancestor in question—no longer finding clay comestible, tried to adapt to other nutriments.

"Europeans have reconstituted an animal bearing a strong resemblance to the Kastéhus; that is the zanglodon, and Cuvier designated it as the ancestor and logical parent of old Adam.[22] But Kastéhus or zanglodon, that being made a great feast of eggs, and did not disdain the fruits that the sun caused to grow on the trees. On that diet, its

---

[22] This is not true; Cuvier never mentioned the zanglodon. As previously noted, it was Camille Flammarion who suggested that the zanglodon might be a saurian ancestor of humankind.

strength diminished and its young were born weaker and weaker, paltry and disinherited.

"But if the solar light put the fecundity of all the Saturnians in peril, their action was doubtless necessary to nature, since Venus caused them to commit the original sin."

"Oh, Madame," Pierre could not help exclaiming, "can you, then, explain the mystery that has so often intrigued my logic?"

"Yes, my child."

"And you will also tell me what baptism and the famous Messianic redemption mean?"

"Yes, but on condition that you don't interrupt me."

"As soon as the Earth had proceeded with the sanitization of its surface by the disappearance of the largest Jupiterian monsters, new stars acted in their turn on the fermentation of the clays of the humus and the waters of the sea. It was the hour of the Shepherd, since it was Venus who came to the aid of those condemned to death.

"No longer finding in their wombs the elements of life necessary to their nymphs, the vivipares attempted the perpetuation of their species by crime. In order to succeed in that, they carried out the most atrocious experiments. And don't smile at the enunciation of that verity, for it's sufficient to read only a few pages of Fabre's *Souvenirs entomologiques* to learn that the birth of a considerable number of insects gives rise to unusual tortures inflicted on innocent creatures; they are required, by their martyrdom, to substitute for the maternal incapacities of the paralyzers and predators.

"Now, nature scarcely varies her methods; what wasps of the *Cerceris* and *Sphex* genera do, the vertebrates have done and continue to do. I remind you, my children, that the Sibyls—and the rare initiates of Paganism as well—knew the secret of Brahma. They related it at length in the three books that the seventh and last pythoness—the Cumaean sibyl—offered to Tarquin the Ancient.[23] She did not believe, on the faith, on the faith of apostles, that the true Messiah was born, and offered to prove it to the Romans, victorious over Greek civilization. Tarquin did not want to study the books, and the Initiate, sensing her physical and mystical death approaching, burned two. The third was saved by an intelligent and subtly-minded Christian, who sent it to Rome, where it enabled the first bishops to present a few great truths in accordance with the apostolic doctrine.

"Paganism died for not having kept the manuscripts of Brahma brought to Orpheus by a Mahana—which is to say by one of the first women deprived of their wings and endowed with legs and matrices. The beings of that epoch still remembered their marine origins, and that is why the pagan religions said that Venus had emerged from the waves.

"I insist on the fact there is nothing down here but females; don't forget that, my children. The ovipare female is designated in the sacred pages under the name of Awaï. She had the shiny brown epidermis of the seals of our day; her head was slender and pretty; her long neck had the grace of plesiosaurs; her fins could serve as wings or paddles at will. As she was fond of the fruits of the

---

[23] In the standard version of the famous legend, of the nine books of prophecy initially offered to the last of the Roman kings, Lucius Tarquinius Superbus (who died in 495 B.C.) by the Sibyl, she burned six before he agreed to purchase the last three; they were placed in the Temple of Jupiter on the Capitoline Hill, but were lost when the Temple was burned in 80 B.C. Tussilia's version seems a trifle anachronistic.

earth, she made use of that double faculty to swoop down on trees and taste fruits forbidden by the Kastéhus. She laid her eggs on the shore, the sun serving as incubator on her behalf, and her children spent their lives as larvae in the Ocean, without allowing themselves to be drawn too far away from the shore. Then, when their gills mutated into bronchi and lungs, when their fins were also transformed, the mothers served as educators of the new generations.

"The Bible is therefore correct when it affirms that our ancestor Eve, or Awaï, did not give birth in pain at one time. But Eve liked fruits, and the legend of the apple has its atom of verity. The Kastéhus females, impotent to nourish their descendancy, initially took advantage of the greed of the awaïs to capture them and make the blood of that marine prey into hydromel for their nurslings. That mode of rearing did not produce excellent results and the Kastéhusian race continued incessantly to decline, all the more so as the frightened awaïs ceded more rarely to their penchant for the fruits.

"They even fasted so willingly that the terrible enemy females were obliged to resolve to nourish their little Kastéhus with eggs on the point of hatching, for which they hunted. The terrestrial nurslings then consumed so many of the products of the eggs that the marine creatures hid their eggs with infinitely more care. There was a period when victory remained faithful to the female ovipare, for a solar cycle. And that would have been the end for the Kastéhus if the demonic Venus had not put her odious spells at the service of the Saturnian animals for a second time.

"She has, until the present day, always saved their existence. The tempting and morbid star, which seems to make dangerous desires flow in the veins of all beings, is the mother of perfumes and savorous fruits. She gave birth to gardens on the edge of the sea, and the Kastéhus hunted the awaïs by night, while the latter, with a heavy flight, succumbed to the temptation, truly placed too close to the waves. Prisoners were taken, whose wings were amputated, and who were kept in the salt-marshes that abounded on the coasts. But captivity diminished their fecundity, to such an extent that, with the aid of Venus, the Kastéhus, urgently needing to ensure the future of their progeniture, went to seek the eggs at source, and deposited their larvae inside the very ovaries of the awaïs.

"The first results were frightful. The Saturnian larvae devoured the unfortunate prisoners alive, and for a long time, every Kastéhus birth cost the life of an awaï. That obliged the terrestrial females to be the prey of a perpetual hunt, of which masculine instinct has retained the taste and the cruelty.

"But one crime led to another. Every terrestrial wanted to reserve the possession of a marine; there were frightful battles between the victors over a pitiable vanquished. They fought over a wretched mutilated individual with more rage than for a treasure. And the law of the strongest—the law of the impotent female, the law of the shameless parasite—was born on our planet and became the universal wound. As the first war, the memory of which was noted in the Brahmin pages took place when the cycle of Mars was at its apogee, the instinct of fratricidal murder was dubbed 'martial.'

"When the sun, having accomplished its evolution, was once again able to bring aid to the victims, however, it gave so much resistant vigor to the awaïs that they no longer died of the bites of the Kastéhus larvae. Certain parts of their bodies atrophied, but their oviduct became strong enough that the parasite could no longer penetrate the envelope. After a long repast of nine months, the new being emerged from the table without having cased the exploited individual to die—but it was then in such a state of inferiority that it was at the mercy of its own victim.

"The awaï gladly avenged herself on the innocent. After several centuries, however, she began to bring into the world strange forms that participated in her race and that of the victor. Then she began to love the children that fate imposed on her, and in her distress, that of an imprisoned and mutilated slave, she hoped for a return to the waves and the aid of her own kind. The ovipares—who gave birth in pain—resembled her in a general fashion, but no longer had wings. On the other hand, they possessed inferior limbs; they could run, whereas their mothers were no longer able to fly or to crawl.

"In secret, they instructed them of the misfortunes of their origin, and as soon as they reached puberty, the young Manhanas—that is what the lamas call the first mammals—fled crying toward the sea, in order to find their ancestors with the long necks and heavy wings. Alas, the grandmothers no longer recognized their granddaughters. The latter swam like them, sang the same chants and spoke about the vanquished and vanished prisoners, but in vain; the awaïs took them for monsters and chased them away with horror.

"The young Kastéhus, although very weak, had no great difficulty in capturing and seizing the young parogenetic hybrids,[24] and thus was created the race of ovo-vivipares, who bear on the forehead the original mark

---

[24] The word *parogénésique* [parogenetic] exists in geology, although not commonly, referring to an enclosure of an older rock in a younger one; it is unclear whether the author has adapted by analogy or resynthesized it from its roots.

of the crime of one species against another. That crime was more odious than a rape, and it is to attenuate the remorse of it that Science, through the mouth of its priests, still allows the woman to hope that she might recover her original form, and might, as before, frolic in the azure, plunge into the bosom of the oceans, and, above all, fulfill her maternal mission without shame and without suffering.

"The age-old instinct is so tenacious that all wise virgins conceive of love as a chaste bliss and a kind of lethargic ecstasy. They retain within them the distant memory of voluptuous hours that their ancestors lived when, after laying their eggs, languid and nonchalant, lying on the golden sand of the strand, they watched the sun incubating heir eggs. In spite of the centuries of evolution of forms and mores, the women of today can never endure the minute of conjugal initiation without an intimate disappointment. Untiringly, they await the Redeemer who will return the beauty and innocence of old to them."

"Oh, I no longer understand!" Pierre protested. "Males and females form a single species today, a well-determined race—there are no more culpables."

"You're speaking lightly, my young friend. There are no more males today than there ever were. There are only terrestrial females, called 'Men,' and marine females, known as 'Women.' The larvae of the Kastéhus ended up being reproduced to microscopic proportions, but they are alive and endowed with movement since, in order to accomplish their metamorphosis, they must travel in the darkness of the maternal organ. In spite of time, in spite of the stars, in spite of civilizations, we have remained the eternal enemies of the Kastéhus, and no birth can be accomplished without the reenactment of the drama of the first age. The Jupiterian always penetrates an egg by force, and battles for a matter of weeks the solar being, in whom nature has ended up nullifying the expulsive strength. The crime is renewed with cunning force and combative force. The two atoms devour one another and the one that is the most vigorous ends up absorbing the vital principle of the other.

"Before arriving at the decisive victory, it is necessary for it to pass through all the states of the past. First it takes on the form of a fish, than that of a toad, and as soon as sex is conquered in the great struggle, it slowly takes on the form of the human nymph such as the centuries, nutriments and climates have fashioned it. Every boy and girl who is born *has already killed*, and that murder is the original sin of which baptism is the symbolic purification. All religions are based on that biological verity; all of them have decreed that a ceremonial ablution will succeed birth.

"Here ends the first sacred lesson."

....

....

....

A great silence reigned, while Madame Wiscorney's meager body was still quivering under the vibration of long chilly frissons. Her respirations, which had been labored for some time, became calmer, and her gaze finally took on the soft gleam that ordinarily rendered it so captivating. A benevolent smile illuminated her face, and her hands—which she had kept nervously clenched, all the fingertips inside—opened in a cordial gesture.

"Well, my children, did the science of the Mahyngas interest you?" she asked, amiably

"For the moment, Madame, it has struck me a formidable sledgehammer blow."

"All pride that is toppled is equally prostrated. Wait for the second lesson, and you will feel that you have a better share. Let's go back home for lunch—which we shall have to take belatedly on several occasions, alas, since noon is the hour of Revelation."

"I no longer dare look at you, my dear fiancée," said Pierre, climbing over one rock after another while following Maya.

"Oh, I still dare, because I'm accustomed to the amazements that Verity reserves for us in all things."

"However…it seems to me that I don't wish you any harm, personally! If I'm hungry for your beauty, for your youth, it's only in order to adore you. I've tried, but I can't discover the instinct of an enemy within me."

"One never discerns them beforehand," riposted the grandmother, cheerfully. "Anyway, enough philosophy for today, young man; go on ahead; run to the pâtissier's, but remember that it was greed that doomed the awaïs."

"I'll fly there," said Pierre, taking the right-hand path."

"I'll swim there," said Maya laughing, who immediately disappeared down the left-hand path.

And Tussilia smiled, for she knew full well that within five minutes the two fiancés would be walking side by side through woods, rocks, brambles and briars.

That was, in fact, what happened, and the dialogue of the two neophytes was soon so amiable and lively that their pace slowed down. They mused so well that when they opened the door of the Villa Ourton they fund the old Hindu sitting before an empty cup and cakes with missing slices.

"Son of the Kastéhus," she said, "I won't entrust my reprovisioning to you."

"All my apologies, Madame."

"I forgive you. Restore yourself and go back to Paris. Read Henri Fabre's theory of parasitism, the chapter on larvae, the chapter on the *Anthrax*, and the one on the metamorphosis of the genus *Meloe*.[25] You'll understand the second lesson of Brahma better, which I shall give you in three days' time. Rendezvous at the Chaos of Yama! And the Truth will dazzle you, my son!"

Pierre inclined over Tussilia's hand, kissed the tips of the priestess' fingers, and accompanied her to the threshold of the laboratory.

Until the moment of departure, he intoxicated himself with Maya's smile, and gently caressed the satined and slightly plump arm of his fiancée with his lips.

"I love you," he repeated, between two inflamed remarks. "Will you love me? Say it again, more forcefully... I adore you."

....
....
....

Maya went to bed extenuated by joy, her flesh weary to the point of depression. It seemed to her that invisible mouths had aspired all her strength, physical and mental. She sought an explanation of the phenomenon, but sleep responded with its mystery to the question mark she posed.

....
....
....

---

[25] *Meloe* is the genus of "oil beetles" or "blister beetles," so called because they release oily droplets when disturbed that contain the toxic chemical cantharidin, also produced by *Cantharis vesicatoria*, or "Spanish fly."

The Second Lesson of Brahma

For five minutes the Initiate had been gathered in an intense concentration, standing in the light, her forehead seemingly made of wax, while her limbs were immobilized in a sort of cataleptic paralysis. Emotional and piously attentive, the two fiancés awaited the promised revelation. Both were wondering, with a certain anguish, whether the gentleness of their tenderness would be able to survive the revelation of the truth.

Pierre could not help regretting the romantic illusion that had bathed his adolescence. He was already no longer very sure of being of superior essence, and he was slightly confused by having to admit that his role was reduced, in sum, to the abuse of muscular force and social laws in order to ensure the survival of his species. What would the words that he was awaiting now annihilate? He felt sad, and pressed his fiancée's hand with a tenderness less conquering.

The sun was radiant, and spangled the ridges of the ricks around them, but no birds were singing in that arid and deserted corner. The melancholy of prehistoric landscapes weighed upon the young people, and it was high time that Tussilia spoke.

At first, the priestess's voice was musical, and this was the text of her lesson:

....
....
....

"The seven days of which the Bible speaks with regard to the creation of the world correspond exactly to seven hundred thousand years of our present calendar, and it was only after that lapse of time that the mammals acquired their almost-definitive forms. Certain bony or cutaneous suppressions in the Kastéhus took long centuries to become hereditary. Their tail, which sustained a kind of mantle floating between the groin and the armpits ended up gradually disappearing, and they also lost two ribs from their thoracic cage—the legend of Eve being taken from Adam's breast has its parcel of truth. The sons of the Kaséhus willingly powder over the facts of history. It's to disguise their maternal inferiority that they have altered Science—the strongest reason is rarely the most sincere.

"Nature having succeeded in creating, crime after crime, a new creature, was not about to leave it unutilized. An impalpable—but nevertheless perceptible—parasite took advantage of the superior qualities acquired by the so-called human race.

"Souls, which, until then, had only had instruments too heavy to manipulate and brains too dense to vibrate, precipitated upon the newborns while the sutures of the skull and the *foramen ovale* were still incomplete. Similarly, they took advantage of the softness of the last vertebrae, which, in that state. Offer little resistance to magnetic implantation."

"Pardon me, Madame, but what is a soul, please?"

"A soul is the nymph of spirit. Spirit is the fire without brightness of the attractive will, cohesive and containing in potency the virtues of lightning. The soul needs, in order to acquire divinity, to extract principles from the fermentation of flesh that are distilled, so to speak, by its Saturnian matrix. Once purified by life, it can return to the bosom of God, the source of unpolluted fire and the cohesive force of the universe.

"Spirit being nothing within us but a distant and arrogant overlord, I only have to instruct you regarding the soul, the parasite of all of us, vivipares and ovipares alike. The soul penetrates within us at the precise moment when the infant emerges from the darkness, pre-sensing the light without yet being able to perceive it. In quest of a permeable and tender body, it is already prowling around the mother in the form of invisible magnetic waves. The latter are supple and radiant elements endowed with three suckers. The first precipitately traverses the scarcely-solidified skull and implants itself in the pineal gland. The second attaches itself to the heart and the third makes sure, by means of a solid support in the coccyx, of dominion over the entire vertebral column. Thus, in a matter of seconds, the soul takes possession of thought, the blood and the nerves. Only the sex organs escape it! And that is the Achilles heel of the soul, which is often endangered by the procreative instinct of the exploited animal."

"May I ask you, Madame, whether animals have a soul to nourish and to enable in its evolution?"

"Yes. The ancients believed that only mammals all had a fluidic parasite. That is why the Egyptians called insects inferior beings. But Brahma thinks differently, for there as many kinds of souls as there are kinds of ovipares. They call elementals those that content themselves with robust instruments and scarcely-circumvoluted brains. On the other hand, it seems that humans have the honor of serving the most advanced parasites, since they enrich the poverty of human animality by materializations of which vegetative life has no need—painting, sculpture and literature, for example. One cannot cite any beast that traces its own silhouette or erects statues. However, many of them live in societies and the spirit of caste is manifest in some."

"Isn't science a psychic emanation?"

"No—many inferior animals seem better informed than humans in that regard. According to Brahma, mechanics, medicine and the principles of architecture are Saturnian instincts, which the terrestrial nymph possesses and confers on the beings issued from its fermentation.

"The soul only gives the sons of the Kastéhus the sacred revelations—those that treat the beyond. It acts on their brains as nature acts on larvae, to enable them to accomplish the gestures necessary for its transformation into a nymph.

"But let us return to the great Verity.

"From its pineal sucker, the soul causes magnetic waves to radiate in the cerebral matter, which arrive after a few days at the eyes, whose gaze they animate. Gradually, it infiltrates the arms and legs, still by means of magnetic roots, and from then on, movements are coordinated and obedient to a will whose primary concern is the security of the spirit for which the soul has responsibility.

"I told you just now that carnal love, with its mystery—which is no longer one for you—escapes the authority of the soul almost completely. The soul can do nothing against the laws of reproduction, and although it deplores them, it is forced to allow them to accomplish the rites of the flesh. Daughters and sons are the nacreous ground that is indispensable to fluidic beings. Being unable to prevent anything, at least the soul can idealize the criminal gesture from which it profits, by allowing a glimpse of the celestial mission that it serves and the fraction of eternity that it contains.

"The sons of the Kastéhus have living atoms within them that aspire to the definitive stage and which, from puberty to adolescence, stifle in the ocean that is reserved to them as a domain. In the same way that the larvae of cockchafers sense variations in the solar temperature from two meters underground, the future Kastéhus sense the approach of the Ovipare susceptible of becoming their prey. Then they revolt and demand their liberty. To obtain it, they boldly trouble the serenity of the body that is their vehicle, and the soul experiences a kind of impatience, but it knows in advance its impotence against the atom, and knows that it is necessary for it to reach an accommodation with matter. The concern for its repose then causes it to commit the worst cowardices. It is that state of the soul of which prostitutes are the most pitiful victims.

"But if the Kastéhus want one prey, the microscopic awaïs want another. Two ferocious appetites solicit one another and confront one another through two bodies nevertheless possessed by the ideal. Then, for two beings deceived by the invisibles of matter, a romance of conquest commences. And the nuptial vertigo often leads them to commit the worst errors—for souls often become disinterested in the future of their own race, and amour is then reduced to desire. It is sufficient to produce a form, but it does not give the actors in that human comedy any of the superior sensualities that true love reserves—and abandonment, indifference and forgetfulness succeed the voluptuousness of embraces. Furthermore, enemy souls can inhabit bodies that have carnal affinities—and then it is hell. The inverse situation does not create more fortunate situations.

"So, in order for two beings to be almost certain of savoring in this world the maximum of happiness reserved for the best of their race, it is only necessary to conclude a reasoned marriage—which is to say, to unite two agreeable forms, enemies that only desire one another more in consequence, which are both exploited by souls of an identical magnetism.

"Then, when the sacred feast is accomplished, when the invisibles of matter have devoured one another and produced one or several forms, the souls will discover between them, in order to struggle against the lassitude of the body, an irresistible and divine attraction, which will be the most intimate and most tender communion of their destiny."

"But Madame, how can only take account of that condition, since the soul is invisible?" said Pierre, desolately.

"The soul is no longer invisible, my child. In the same way that the microscope reveals destructive and constructive microbes every day, certain laboratory apparatus reveals, without contact, the qualities of density, clarity and iridescence of every soul that approaches it. Shortly, you will be able to convince yourself of the truth of that affirmation. In any case, if, instead of teaching children a host of useless things, they were made to undertake certain psychic exercises, a large number of humans would be able to see their contemporaries' auras."

"It's true, then, that mediums can see light radiating from certain people?"

"Why not, my friend? The saints radiated such beautiful light the religion coifs them all with a golden aureole. Saints are only human. Yellow is, in fact, the dominant color among the spiritual, blue indicates idealism, violet reveals intellectuals and red altruists."

"You're joking, Madame!"

"Think, my friend, that even terrestrial electricity, following the course of its current, appears in the most various colors. Why should animal magnetism not have the same power, in accordance with the flesh or the thought that dominates it? Since you will shortly see your own soul, admit the principle for a moment and apply it to judge the nature of the nascent love that attracts you to Maya."

"Oh, Madame, don't destroy my joy," the young man implored. "I love my fiancée so much!"

"Your sincerity is beyond doubt, Pierre; but it's necessary that you make sure today of the harmony of your souls, because...Maya's happiness depends on the realization of a prophecy. You know that her beauty magnetizes your desire, but you're no longer unaware that that beauty serves as pasture to the starvelings that you carry in your loins. You have also learned that, in spite of the softness of your kisses and the intoxication of your embrace, Maya can do nothing about the outcome of the obscure battles engaged in her entrails between the parasites and the Solar Being of which she is the true female. The latter might not allow herself to be devoured. It is therefore necessary that your two souls accept, without reticence, the best and the worst of the destiny of your two biological entities. And you will know that she accepts it in advance if, when she brings you close to the psychic sphere in a little while, holding you by the hand, red, livid or brown lights do not traverse your aura.

"Remember, Maya, the bird that came to alight, palpitating and overcome, before the serpent, its executioner. You will know the anguish of a similar intoxication. Your body will be bitten and vampirized by infinitely tiny enemies. That is the nuptial feast. But if your souls have the same ideal of beauty and flight, you will know, during and after the original crime, the ecstasy of magnetic nymphs still without puberty. They will reserve for the children issued from your embraces parasites of the same essence as themselves. For you that will be simple, complete and durable happiness, and you will give birth to the individual, male or female, with will redeem humankind."

"Madame!" exclaimed Pierre. "I swear to love Maya until death...but what is death? The fatality that limits my amour?"

"You should have deduced that from these two lessons, my son. The soul, parasitic on the body, grows, embellishes and evolves to the detriment of the flesh whose energies it inspires. Even the souls that, wisely, do not abuse the magnetic appetite, fatally exhaust the vital sources of the cells that compose us. That is old age. Then, when the stage of necessary growth arrives, they break their three attachments more or less rapidly. That is death.

"After that separation from matter, they float in the sir, diaphanous and imperceptible to the eyes of nymphs. The fly is not perceived by the mole sniffing the air before the storm, but the dipteron exists nevertheless. Once free, the soul has to reproduce; it then offers the spiritual equivalent of our material beauty—which is to say, the more or less dazzling aura that ours actions have variously colored. The body still lives after the departure of the magnetic being; the heart still beats—but three invisible wounds allow the cohesive force of the cells to escape, and death does its work of decomposition. Only two souls that have loved one another through two enemy bodies, two souls that have made instruments of spiritual life of two necessary hatreds, find one another again and continue on the astral plane the dream of tenderness that they have sketched on earth. The old age of a happy couple has to have the same tenderness and serenity as the mystical engagement...

"And now, my young friends, run to my laboratory; the amometer is ready. Maya knows how to operate it. If your colors complete one another, amplify one another in radiance, you must both be here again in three days. Go, children! And may destiny be affirmed! I'll come back at dusk; I need to pray."

....

....

....

This time, the young couple walked along the pathways silently and gravely. Instead of seeking one another out, their gazes were evasive, for they both feared the precision of the imminent experiment. Were their two souls allied or tolerant?

So much sadness weighed upon their hearts that Maya burst into sobs, and Pierre, torn himself by an immense dolor, put his arm around the young woman, who wept softy, in little hiccups, upon his breast.

"Console yourself, my adored one; even if the unknown guest that lives within me does not have the same high quality as yours, I shall strive to ameliorate it, to elevate it; it's necessary for me to sustain and retain your love, isn't it, Maya?"

"Have no fear! In spite of all hostilities, I shall remain yours!"

"My love!"

For a long time they remained thus, sadly enlaced. Then, almost without relaxing their grip, they went on, his to hip, shoulder to shoulder, their cheeks so close that the tears flowing from the eyes of one of them moistened both faces.

An infinite softness emanated from their common terror, and without expressing it, each was thinking: *It would really be too cruel if so much tenderness might be born from two unsympathetic souls.*

The path of the Solitaire being the shortest way back, they took it, and, as if their bruised joy already had need of the balm of memory, Maya designated from a distance the Absorbed Rock.

"That's where you said 'I love you' to me for the first time."

"Let's go repeat it in the same place, under the gaze of the Immured."

Soon, they were both standing, enlaced and melancholy, before the stone mask with the troubling pupils. But the light of the June afternoon was filtered in such a way that it even put an amiable and tender shadow into the sunshine hollows. Looking at the eyes sculpted in the rock, Maya exclaimed: "But its gaze is benevolent and encouraging today!"

Who can ever tell what source of energy their might be in the most puerile of superstitions? Because the stone was bathed by soft and lukewarm sunbeams, it seemed to the two fiancés that misfortune could no longer reach them. And without further delay, they hastened toward Tussilia's laboratory.

Along in that place of study, with test-tubes, retorts, serpentines and piles for witnesses, a final apprehension paralyzed them momentarily.

Eventually, Maya made the contact, and, as simply as anything in the world, as if she were dealing the cards at bridge, she said:

"There's my soul."

Pierre Montala could not help uttering an exclamation of surprise. The phenomena of luminosity at a distance, and the sparks, and finally, the coloration of the crystals enclosed in the glass sphere, amazed him. However, as the spectacle of a decisive experiment was still impending, without any scene-setting, he replied: "What? That's all it is, a soul? A glow?"

"Yes, but a glow that passes through any insulation. A glow that becomes iridescent in accordance with the intensity of the magnetism emitted. Look what happens in response to the approach of my arm, and then my head."

On reflection, confronted by the orange-tinted light that radiated from his companion's forehead and hair, Pierre soon understood the importance of the scientific discovery that had been given to him for experimentation. Convinced, he cried, delightedly: "I believe! I believe! Your soul is beautiful, Maya! Let's see mine."

Slowly, Pierre advanced his fingertips, and his emotion was great when he saw the sphere light up with pink and emerald fires.

"No dark patches!" exclaimed the young woman, clapping her hands. "Let's put our hands together, then."

How they trembled with delightful emotion, those two young and beautiful beings, requesting of the flameless and smokeless fire the judgment of their destiny! What a sublime legend there were living, leaning over the sphere of the Brahmanic initiates!

For a moment, the sizzle of the terrestrial electricity became a crackle, and long white flames traversed the apparatus; but orders was soon restored to everything, and calcium crystals were marbled with the most beautiful green, the purest violet and the brightest red imaginable.

"So...?" said Pierre, so joyful that he could no longer find words.

"Well, yes!" the young woman exulted. "We can love one another—but that's not all. It's necessary for you to submit to the proof of the magic tube."

"What's that?"

"The most troubling psychic discovery of all. Look at this crystal tube, into which, after removing all the air it contained, that pinch of powder the color of mastic was introduced. Study it attentively. It's dull and banal. I simply pick it up, without putting it in contact with any current. Look!"

In less than two seconds, in Maya's hands, the dull powder was illuminated, shining with silver-white gleams, lightly streaked with mauve. When, as if playing with it, she caused the contents of the tube to move from one end and the apparatus to the other, sparks sprang from the precipitated atoms.

"Your turn," said the young woman, putting the glass wand down on the table. Wait until there's no more trace of luminosity in the grains of matter."

After a few seconds, Pierre gripped the tube between his palms, and the colorless powder lit up, with magnificent blue gleams.

"Obviously," he said, "each person radiates waves of a different color. The experiment is peremptory, for no external agent collaborates in the phenomenon of illumination. You see me confused..."

"And convinced?"

"Of our future happiness? Yes, Maya. Let our sacred parasites live," he concluded, putting his arms round his fiancée.

"Yes, but those that aren't sacred? I shall be their victim."

"Forgive the death that I carry in my flesh, my darling, and accept, for the life that we're going to create, all my courage, all my endeavor, and the chaste love of my thought."

"Pierre!"

"Maya!"

Their eyes drowned in an extreme ecstasy, the fiancés, sure henceforth of their future, hugged one another, and did not speak for a long time. They felt incapable of translating the solemnity of the moment, for if their bodies were experiencing the glad lassitude of past anguishes, they sensed soft and tender mystical alleluias singing within them. And they listened to the occult vibrations that summarized, in a divine language, the word of release and triumph:

"Finally."

....

....

....

The Third Lesson of Brahma

The weather was less beautiful than during the first two Brahmic lessons. Heavy clouds, sable in color, were rising above the horizon, and as, for the most part, the rocks in the Chaos of Yama affected the vague contours of fantastic beasts, the stifling vapor rising from the ground seemed to be giving breath to those stone monsters.

When Tussilia got up to introduce her final revelation with the sacred chant that she had sung twice before, Maya, who was extremely nervous, could not suppress a certain tremor in her fingers and eyelids.

Nevertheless, the old woman, began:

....

....

"You know the laws that rule your bodies, haunted by enemies, and your souls, fortunately of friendly races. For the moment, the illogicality of that duality does not seem very oppressive to you, but life will take responsibility for demonstrating to you the extremes to which it can extend.

"All the surprises of amour come from the diversity of species of the souls that inhabit human bodies. And that affirmation is not surprising if one refers, for example, to the astonishing number of predators that paralyze the same species of caterpillars or grasshoppers. All those victims of totally different beings are subjected to a similar torture. Among souls, two races in particular share the majority of individuals: one that envelops its spirit in an intense magnetic cocoon and one that neglects the dare of that fluidic envelope.

"The first of these parasites generally, but not exclusively, takes the bodies of women for its field of action. It accommodates itself to precarious forces and excessive nervousness. The second preferentially selects masculine forms, and it is right to do so, for the spirit, poorly insulated by the thin fluidic layer, imposes a vigorous suction on its victim, who needs a robust constitution to resist it. But I repeat that there are numerous errors at the moment of the implantation of the soul.

"I have told you that souls are all too often indifferent to the act of amour, which escapes their domination. Some of them, however, often amuse themselves with the emotion that the adventure of desire can cause magnetic larvae that are not of the same race as themselves. Have you re-read, Pierre, the story of the *Anthrax* larvae?"

"Yes, Madame. With nothing but brief and repeated kisses, the worm of the *Anthrax* empties out that of the *Chalicodoma*,[26] even though it is larger and more powerful. The latter allows itself to be consumed without resistance, and the crime is accomplished without any wound or sore. No mean of exit is visible, but all the living matter of the *Chalicodoma* passes into the body of the *Anthrax*, and each worm repeats that murder several times before mutating into a nymph."

"All the incoherencies of amour are explained by that mode of conquest, generally dear to the sons of the Kastéhus. My children, the heavy souls favor the nuptial chase by means of the contribution of a superior and intensive will. The kiss is the sucker of attachment that aspires the resistance of instinct in the female. It is thus, af-

[26] *Chalicodoma* is a genus of bees that includes the largest of all bee species; some wasp species of the *Anthrax* genus specialize in parasitizing its larvae.

ter a few chaste caresses, that wise virgins surrender or offer themselves to the enemy's tragic feast."

"However, Madame, there are many young women who derive a keen pleasure for those liberal associations."

"I don't dispute that; it proves that the Anthrax-soul, if I may designate the Don-Juanesque soul thus, can succeed by means of the kiss in hypnotizing the more precious and least well-armed soul. The man profits from that magnetic lethargy to operate the deposit of his larvae. He acts in the fashion of the paralyzers, but his venom is purely psychic.

"I am not seeking, in this explanation of a verity, to put an entire sex on trial. When it is a matter of uniting two existences, it is very important to verify the luminosity of the two fiancés. I hold that precaution to be as necessary as the medical examination of two spouses. The work of the flesh being the satisfaction of two hatreds that are slaking themselves in joy, the reaction to that joy is always lassitude and bitterness. It is therefore necessary that the two souls, promised at the same feast, make appeal to all their philosophy in order not to be tempted to hold one another reciprocally responsible for the quotidian misfortunes that are going to assail them."

"One last question," said Pierre, whose lucidity was making him more audacious since he no longer had to fear losing Maya. "If I've understood correctly, life is nothing but an uninterrupted sequence of rapes. Every being lives between two parasites, one material and the other spiritual. Whence comes, then, the instinct of liberty that exalts us, and the free will that all religions promise us?"

"No one is free, since the universal harmony is the implacable Order in which individuality is a myth. What is important down here is the future of the Being that the earth encloses. All the rest is the effervescence of debris.

In any case, if social conventions did not inhibit the free expansion of nature, we would be less rebellious. Individuals are so well equilibrated between the demands of their various parasites that they give the name of liberty to the need to escape any constraint that might inconvenience theirs fluidic or material exploiters.

"Humans curse the civilization that inhibit their amorous acts, and have no sooner accomplished them than scruples or commentaries spoil the memory of their voluptuousness. Only one thing generally survives the various eddies that stir human instincts, and that is the cult of Beauty. One senses the harmony of lines and their extrapolation into the infinite, and that the future of magnetic beings is linked to the nobility of form. Religions have misunderstood the importance of the body in the evolution of the spiritual parasite. It is necessary neither to scorn it not glorify it, but the accord it the cares that it has the right to expect of everyone. To rejoice in the grace and vigor it possesses is perfectly legitimate; but not to take care of its health, compromising the life of the cells that compose us, is a double crime, for it afflicts the two parasites whose existence our forms are charged with ensuring.

"Verity often emerges from the pens of rhymers, one of whom has said that gazes are the kisses of the soul. In the kisses of souls, always forming fluidic suckers, a gaze may get a grip on a will that is not on the defensive, especially if the solar seed obsesses a woman with urgent aspirations.

"And now that, by means of precisions, I have battered a breach in the capital errors with which literature of religion have made a shroud for the sacred Verity, I finally arrive at the end of my mission, which is to reveal to you your predestination.

"Nothing that I have said to you will weigh upon your youth, because nothing can impede nature in the monotonous exercise of the nuptial vertigo. In haste to prepare nymphs, vowed to the hatching of souls, you will live as banal and tender a romance as can be desired. But however modest your actions might be and however gray your existence, you will remember my words, and from you will emerge the Redeemer awaited by humans and by the unknown guests. You are going to bear the burden of a terrible glory, and..."

Absorbed by the attention he was paying to Tussilia's words, Pierre had not seen that his fiancée had gone pale a moment ago, that her body had taken on a cataleptic rigidity and that her lovely smile was traversed by dolorous contractions.

"Refuse! Refuse, Pierre!" she cried. "I'm afraid! Kacyapa is sending me the reflection of a tragic image! The future... The future... I don't want it...I don't want it. Pity! Pity! Refuse, Pierre!"

"No one can struggle against Kacyapa, my child," said the Hindu. "All causality comes from him, and every effect has been ordered for a century of centuries. Remember the principal phases of life that have been shown to you. Day by day, in the determined simplicity of great things, you are telling the beads of the rosary of your Predestination. For a long time, nothing will seem to mark your personality. Nothing will distinguish you from the crowd—but remember that Brahma was a savant of very ordinary aspect, that Cakya Mouni begged, that the sibyls were like other women, and that on the day when Jesus was born, he was just a crying, disinherited baby like all the rest, although he was to overturn the Roman colossus. The Redeemer that Brahma announces must be brought to earth by the winged being born of you..."

At that moment, a sob tore Maya's throat, and almost immediately, her limbs resumed their flexibility. Her eyelids, closed until then, parted, and Pierre was disturbed by the fear legible in her gaze.

"What's the matter, my love?"

"I've seen," she said, huddling against him.

"What? Tell me, quickly."

But the young woman had pulled herself together, under the flash that sprang from Tussilia's eyes.

"I apologize," she murmured, "and I'll listen to the expected prophecy with all the respect that I owe you, Grandmother."

Pierre no longer knew what to think or do. His imagination was floating between dream and reality; the actions and gestures of the two women, which troubled him in various ways, anesthetized his logic and his instinct of contradiction. In any case, the clouds were heaping up above their heads, and it was wiser not to delay the conclusion of the last lesson of Brahma. However, an enormous weight seemed to be weighing on his heart, for he sensed that Maya was holding back, with great difficulty, the explosion of an immense despair.

It was, therefore, in a heavy and menacing material and mental atmosphere that Tussilia went on.

"The time has come when, under the influence of Mars, millions of men are about to kill one another, hatefully, at a distance. Charnel houses will be displayed under the sun, and that star will cause a destructive atom to bloom pitilessly. It will kill as many millions by means of the infinitely small as by the gigantic engines of war.

"But the wings that the Kastéhus hoped to obtain by their hybridization with the awaïs will be replaced by artificial wings. In the Martian struggle, they will obtain the impetus necessary to launch them outside the atmospheric envelope and attain the cradle of the promised Redeemer.

"The King of the World, whose realm is subterranean, affirms that he will introduce himself as a son of the heavens, mounted on an aircraft. His first act will be to impose the universal science and love of which all believers dream. That love, according to him, will only be able to spring from an intensive culture of light and brilliant soul.

"But I am a disciple of Brahma, and I affirm this: it is necessary that a man, or a woman, equipped with artificial wings, shall risk himself or herself in interplanetary space and bring back the being of light that will destroy all darkness, all doubt and all futile mystery. The love of that being—which our present ignorance cannot foresee—will be the virgin mother of superhumans that all religions await. The sons of the Kastéhus, having become sterile, will enter then into legend. But between now and then, more tears will flow from the eyes of mothers than drops of rain will fall upon these rocks.

"Nevertheless, my son, there is still time for you to deny your love. If I have not convinced you, if you will one day mock the revealed Truth, do not cross the threshold of the Villa Ourton. Now that you know, you should only enter my house in divine promise. Alas, another will soon come in malign promise, but that one has nothing to do with my mission."

For their only response, Pierre and Maya, having looked at one another, embraced one another. Their impulse was so irresistible that the old Initiate bowed her head, softened.

"Will the destiny of one be the destiny of the other?" she asked.

"Yes, Madame."

"Yes, my Lia."

"Then receive the swastika of the Predestined.[27] It has been sent to me by the Dalai Lama of Lhasa. May Kacyapa and Bromhyda protect you!"

....
....
....
....
....

Tussilia had scarcely finished speaking than a diluvian downpour fell upon the forest. In spite of the advanced awning provided by three overlapping blocks of stone, the water formed a stream, which came with the impetuosity of a torrent to put the sandals of the three occultists to the proof.

"Well," said Pierre, laughing, "if humankind must weep tomorrow as much as the heavens today, I wonder what can be going to happen to it?"

....
....
....

The storm having exhausted its fury rapidly, the sun gazed between two beautiful gilded clouds at the forest of Fontainebleau, and the fiancés, leaping from rock to rock, took the route to Barbizon again, playing like two fawns at liberty.

---

[27] The author had no way of knowing, obviously, that the reputation of the swastika, a sacred symbol in both Buddhism and Hinduism, would soon be soiled by the most martial of all the sons of the Kastéhus. The Sanskrit root of the term means "auspicious," which is why it is being presented to the Predestined progenitor of the Redeemer.

Suddenly, Pierre retraced his steps, leaving Maya on the path, nonplussed. He rejoined Tussilia, who was marching serenely, and greeted him with a smile.

"Madame, you have revealed unusual mysteries to me, but I can sense nothing within me that advertises any favorable sign whatsoever."

"My child, Brahma, Buddha and Jesus, three divine emanations, had no presentiment at first of their future glory."

"Thank you, Madame. I'll go and embrace Maya, to express all my gratitude to you."

"How very French of you!" Tussilia approved.

....
....
....
....
....

When they arrived at the Villa Ourton, the priestess and her two neophytes had the pleasant surprise of finding Madame d'Angeville, Ghislaine and Louis Dubar in the drawing room. After the initial effusions, the dowager struck a somewhat solemn pose, and declared in a triumphant voice:

"My dear Madame, I have the honor of announcing to you the official engagement of our granddaughter with Monsieur Louis Dubar, advocate. It is the union of two matching families, two equal fortunes and two young persons imbued with the same morality and the same virtues."

"Oh, you little secret-keeper, you didn't tell me anything about your idyll," said Maya, embracing her twin sister.

"A well brought-up young woman leaves to her parents the concern of occupying themselves with her heart," put in the paternal grandmother. "And what about you, Maya—it will be necessary for me to occupy myself with finding a husband for you too, for Prince Charmings no longer go riding in the forests."

"Destiny has no need of anyone," riposted Madame Wiscorney, "and the proof is that for a quarter of an hour, my darling has been engaged to Monsieur Pierre Montala. It will be the union of two healthy young people, two luminous souls and two frank, loyal and alert tendernesses."

There was, naturally, a mutual exchange of congratulations, handshakes and motional kisses. Then, a fine appetite gathered six individuals radiant with happiness, albeit very dissimilar, around a table flourishing with good China tea, cream and Samos wine.

The rain was hammering against the windows, but no one cursed the tempest, for in a house where dreams are palpitating, nothing augments the sentiment of bliss like the vain efforts of the unchained elements outside.

Montala and Dubar only went back to their hotel as midnight approached. Barbizon was asleep, all shutters closed, so Pierre and Louis were able to talk without fear of indiscreet ears as they went past all the marble plaques evoking the glory of the school of 1830.[28]

"So you've got yourself caught too, my dear Montala," said the young Dubar. "It's a risk we run! And

---

[28] "L'École de 1830" [the school of 1830], was a term coined in 1907 by Johannès Plantadis in an article on "Les Maîtres du paysage limousin" [The Masters of the Limousin Landscape], identifying a group of artists aggregated in the vicinity of Barbizon, including Jules and Victor Dupré, Louis Cabal, Constant Troyon, Fernand Chaigneau and Léon Fleury, who became key associates of Millet and Rousseau's École de Barbizon.

since it's written, I'm quite content to have you as a brother-in-law."

"Me too," replied Pierre, courteously, "but I don't know whether you're joking or serious."

"One is always serious when it's a question of marriage. I would, however, have preferred..."

"You can't have imagined, though, that Mademoiselle Ghislaine would have become your mistress?"

"It wouldn't have taken much. I maneuvered well; our romance flourished in myrrh, incense and melted candles; it was delightfully exciting."

"But?"

"Well, yes, there was a *but*. To begin with, I studied the child at a few formal balls. I slipped the most irresistible amorous clichés that Don Juan and Paul Bourget have invented into her ears, and as I'm able to read the eyes of virgins troubled by spring, I attempted the conquest of the pious young woman. I must confess that the game of audacities and timidities was so expert that I burned like a simple candle lit before the Madonna."

"So you don't love your fiancée?"

"Yes, I love her...or rather, I desired her madly, because her possession was difficult. Now, she's much less interesting; I'll have her without a struggle, without cunning, and that victory doesn't enthuse me."

"You're haunted by the instinct of hunting and rape."

"There's truth in that. What is a woman? An inferior being, no? Exquisite as gallant prey, but who, in marriage, can only play the role of doll. Unless she contents herself with that of housekeeper..."

"And that of mother? You don't think about that?"

"O, very little, very little. If Ghislaine is maladroit, so much the worse for her. Besides which, I've told her that I don't like children, and it's understood that she'll prefer the slenderness of her figure and the bloom of her complexion."

"You've dared to raise that subject with a young woman?"

"Don't be so naïve. You know very well that one says even more cynical things between two forbidden kisses. While everyone believed that Ghil was at mass, I took her to my place. She defended her body, but I had all the time in the world to fashion her mind before her governess discovered the ruse."

"You don't have any remorse?"

"That's a joke. They only had to keep a closer eye on her. And the proof that audacity pleases women is that if one didn't keep a close eye on them they'd all—all, you hear—be dangling from our bell-ropes."

"On that point, my dear, you're in error. They aren't being protected, only being hindered a little by hypocrisy, but rather being pushed to abandonment. They're ignorant of all realities and everything is ingenious in needling their nerves and their curiosity in the direction of amour. They want to know what's being hidden from them; we'd do the same in their place. Maya knows everything—and because she knows, it would be futile to attempt a dishonest adventure."

"The little witch knows everything? Well, that's scarcely amusing for you, my dear. Fortunately between theory and practice..."

"There's still room for disappointment..."

"Oh, as to that, my dear...it's necessary to learn your métier. No woman leaves my arms disappointed."

"I don't confuse pleasure, which can always by simulated, with true love."

"Romantic! Love with its sentimental tralala, like religion, is good for women; it occupies them and creates the moral sufferings that are indispensable to them. It's true that poets also like the sensuality of tears, but I thought you were more manly than that. A sportsman, a hearty fellow like you! Bah! I'll teach you a thing or two, my dear brother-in-law. Did you have much difficulty with your parents regarding this marriage?"

"A little."

"Not me. The family's honorable, the girl charming, the dowry appreciable."

"Oh, there's a dowry? My father didn't say anything to me about that. He only told me that he'd give me a job in his business at twenty-five thousand francs a year."

"You're being mounted on a pin. There's three hundred thousand by contract. Above all, demand community of wealth!"

"I'm not making a business deal."

"For a man, marriage is always a business deal; don't play the angel. Wings don't come cheap. Anyway, here we are at the hotel."

"Good night, Monsieur Irresistible."

"Good night, candid and serene poet."

"What do you mean?"

Without waiting for a reply, Pierre burst into youthful and tolerant laughter; then he went up to his room.

While waiting for sleep, he could not help murmuring: "A month ago, I thought almost the same as him, and now...am I really convinced? Perhaps not...but so troubled...I can never think again as I once did. The Redeemer will have a rude task, to extirpate all the errors that have been imagined as truths..."

....
....
....

During the first three weeks of July 1914. Ghislaine delighted in her dangerous illusions.

"He loves me…he loves me, and I can make of him what I like," she said to her sister. "I gaze at him, smile at him, and he'll never be able to live without me. Then again, he desires me with such fervor that he doesn't want to afflict my beauty. We'll only have children later, much later, when we've exhausted the gamut of voluptuousness. For everything is permitted in marriage, and I want to be the ever-new and always adored mistress."

The young woman intoxicated herself for hours with the enormous stupidities that impotent intellectuals have written about pleasure. Of the soul, the ideal, duty, there was never any question, for in order to make one forget the prosaicism and cruelty of the nuptial rape, the classic maneuver is to stupefy the virginal mind with the most excessive literary tirades. Unconsciously, Ghislaine mingled the Gospel with novels, and her grandmother swooned, tenderized, before the absurdity, either perverse or naïve, of her assertions.

At the official dinners that were held at the Villa Ourton, the Montala, Dubar and d'Angeville families felt animated by a real sympathy toward one another. There was very human conversation regarding the sacred union. In fact, the dowager d'Angeville, seconded by Madame Montala, who had not laid down her arms, won all the newcomers over to their opinion, and they mocked the old lady in chorus, who appeared not to suspect it. It is necessary to agree, in fact, that the Initiate's attitude was singular. She often came back from the forest with her face so pale that one might have thought her a corpse. Once or twice, she took Pierre and Maya into the underwood, and the two fiancés came back with their eyes swollen with tears and their gazes desperate.

One evening, the dowager Madame d'Angeville, having struck her most sententious pose, declared: "We're all of the opinion that Ghislaine and her sister ought to marry on the same day. It would be picturesque, and—why not confess it—also more economical."

"I don't have any objection to that," Tussilia replied.

"Yes, but..." The three women's smiled became pinched. "There's Maya's atheism, which impedes the plan."

"Atheists don't believe in God," Maya replied. "Grandmother and I bless him in all his works. I love and venerate him."

"Hmm! You also pray to him, perhaps?"

"If praying is requesting, I don't pray to him; but if prayer is expressing one's admiration and resigning oneself to the laws he has established, I pray to him."

"Then why don't you go to church?"

"A truce on religious discussion," Tussilia cut in, gravely. "I've said and I repeat that if Pierre demands it, Maya may embrace the Catholic religion. That's not of any importance."

Three exclamations responded to that declaration, and three voices yapped in chorus: "Not of any importance! On the contrary, it's the only important thing in life."

"What are you complaining about, then? Since I've acted in such a way as not to hinder any conviction, Maya can have herself baptized whenever you like, but it's futile to press the point."

"Why, if you please?"

"Because our children's marriage isn't imminent."

"You're losing your mind, Madame; my son will marry Ghislaine in September."

"And mine..."

"Yours will not marry Maya for another four years, Madame."

"Has Beelzebub fixed that date for you?" sniggered Madame Montala.

"Perhaps," said the Hindu, smiling. "War will be unleashed in ten days, and as the Kaiser, as a malign Initiate, believes that he can changes destiny by the strength of arms, putting off the fatal date by a year, the struggle will be terrible, disconcerting, long and discouraging. What ruins! What mourning!"

"No," said Louis Dubar, "there won't be a war. If you were right, the stock market would have gone down, and it's holding firm."

"Certainly not," said Montala senior, supportively. "The military supply chain would be making provision, and they're not."

"Then again, God wouldn't permit such a horror," concluded Madame d'Angeville.

"God has no concerns, no stocks and shares, and no suppliers," the Hindu insisted. "The hour of martial fury has sounded; that is the only certainty, and I weep with all my heart for the young men of Europe."

That evening, Tussilia's guests scarcely shook her hand. She heard the sardonic and malevolent laughter that the three old ladies exchanged under her roof...but without any emotion, she went to her laboratory and spent the rest of the night there.

....
....
....
....
....

It was in Paris, at Madame Montala's house, that the fiancés and their relatives were due to dine on the day of mobilization. All day long, Pierre and Louis, like all those of their age, had been prowling around the famous white posters striped with blue, white and red. Their fathers had paced for long hours like caged beasts, tugging their meager moustaches, no longer all-conquering. But it was necessary to put on a brave face and all the men tried to do so. The young ones, while buying cases for uniforms, launched quips, crying: "To Berlin by berline!" and a thousand other stupidities, because anguish in never witty.

....

....

None of the guests at Auteuil was late, and when the maid came to announce that dinner was served, Ghislaine was stuffing Louis Dubar's pockets with sashes and medallions imprinted with prayers. Pierre and Maya were looking at each other without saying a word. The fathers were telling stories about the German marmalade they had made in '70, and the mothers—livid, as if stunned by misfortune—were talking in low voices in order to struggle against the sobs that were making their voices hoarse. Naturally, there was no talk at table of anything but the war.

"My opinion is that the mobilization is a bluff," the advocate repeated. "The Bourse is firm, damn it! And then, it would be stupid to fight, to arrive fatally at general ruination. I don't believe it. We'll put on our little military parade, and everyone will go home."

"You're right," said Madame Montala, "it's a bluff. God won't permit people, sat the level of civilization we've reached, to slaughter one another as in the times of Attila. The Germans aren't barbarians, and Heaven will save our children."

"God's designs are impenetrable," added Madame d'Angeville.

"Yes, but our flesh is very penetrable," Pierre joked.

"Shut up! Shut up!" cried his mother. "That idea drives me mad. It's necessary to trust in the Almighty. I'll pray! Pray! Won't you all pray with me, Mesdames?" she implored, her gaze making a tour of her guess.

Unfortunately, her eyes encountered Tussilia's calm and pitying. Immediately, one of the iniquitous fits of anger to which the war was to give rise in millions, burst in the heart of the desperate mother.

"But now I think of it, how did Madame Wiscorney know, and was able to tell us with so much precision, ten days ago, that war would be unleashed on this very day? What acquaintances do you have down here? With demons or with men? If it's with Hell, may God forgive you, but if it's with men, it's more serious. Only spies are so well-informed."

"Maman!" said Pierre. "Are you losing you mind? You're insulting a saintly woman."

"A saint? A saint? Get away—a debauchee, a witch, capable of anything! Yes, of anything except protecting our children! The Church says that a witch can unleash death, but she can't save anyone. Look at this one—she's powerless even to protect the happiness of her granddaughter."

"Can your Jesus do any better than her?" riposted Maya's fiancé, losing his patience.

A second of silence and stupor brought the nerves of the mistress of the house to paroxysm. Finding no reply, she uttered a scream, and started trembling in her every limb. The crisis that shook her thereafter was such that she had to be taken away, shouting at the top of her voice: "A spy, that woman? A witch!"

Then, the universal consternation prolonged the silence around the table.

Tussilia, however, in spite of the apologies that Pierre and Monsieur Montala lavished upon her, did not want to remain under the insult of the malevolent words that had just been pronounced. The Dubars and the d'Angevilles tried in vain to persuade her that the words of a sick woman could not afflict her; she demanded a categorical and immediate explanation. Impassive and imperious, she installed herself in an armchair in the drawing-room, and everyone understood that nothing could any longer prevent the clash of two mysticisms.

It was nearly eleven o'clock when Madame Montala made her reentry into the family circle. She was pale, and leaning on the arm of her son, with whom it was manifest that a supreme argument must have taken place. When she had sat down, Tussilia stood up. Never had her silhouette emanated so much majesty. Never had her gaze radiated more light, and never had her voice seemed so softly harmonious.

"Madame," she said, "I forgive you for the reckless language that has troubled this union, but as the malady that has seized you by the throat tonight will become epidemic after tomorrow, I want to be sheltered from all suspicion. Soon, in fact, everyone who thinks differently from his neighbor will be held to be a traitor or a spy. I am neither one nor the other, but *I know*. To betray, it is necessary to doubt, for one always betrays in favor of the one that one supposes to be the stronger."

"But in sum, what do you know?" a voice put in.

"That the war is eternal, or, rather, that it will be, so long as the cocoon of humus has not burst. Between now and then, whatever utopians, prophets and Christs might say, humans being overabundant on earth, it is necessary, indispensable, and hence fatal, that men will kill their brethren. The need to kill, for the Promised Land, dates from the second islet to emerge from the waves.

"All the celestial envoys have used that irresistible image, because every animal drawn from the primal clay wants the earth, the whole earth, and the earth forever! Before the Canaan of Moses there was the Ural of Orpheus, as there was Colchis for the Argonauts, the Occident for the Goths.

"At any rate, when one cannot excite homicidal instincts with the lure of a few arpents of land to conquer, one makes them kill for a place in the Elysian Fields. That is the Promised Land that has inspired the worst torments and caused the greatest number of human beings to die."

"Madame, you're overstepping...."

"Let me speak! Land acquired or Promised Land, that is the trap which nature sets for martial fury. And nothing in the world is more tragic than the suicide of bodies accepted by their souls. There are microbes and there is old age, which have already tried to maintain a perpetual equilibrium between birth and death, but as those destructions are insufficient, the souls themselves, pressed by martial vibrations, become deliriously excited, and to the detriment of their own fate, send forms rushing against forms. Millions and millions of men are going to perish."

"Pierre!"

"Louis!" groaned the two mothers.

"Death will gorge itself on blood. It has perfected its weapons and can kill in a cowardly fashion, invisibly and at a distance; there will be an eternal slaughterhouse! The very clouds will become the accomplices of the fire and poison that the Lucifers will launch upon innocents. At any rate, this war will be the last."

"Ah! Finally..."

"Yes, for in the next cycle of Mars there will be a pitiless and universal slaughter," Tussilia went on

"That's not true! That's not true! Madame, Jesus has said: 'Love one another!'"

"And he had been impotent to establish that love, because that love would be harmful to the sacred nymph. Too many men...there are too many men..."

"What you are saying is monstrous, Madame! Fortunately, you are the only woman who dares to think of such horrors," said Monsieur Dubar senior, indignantly.

"What did I tell you—she's a demon!"

"I am, indeed, the only woman who can dare to *tell* the truth. But you shall see whether your mothers, your wise virgins and your wives will not act in the same fashion tomorrow. I'm not talking here about the best, of those whom you name, with good reason, saints, great French-women, heroic women. Well, every young woman is going to demand that the man she loves should 'do his duty'—which is to say that he should go to his death, with a smile still on his lips. You will see the scornful gazes that they will direct against cowards and deserters. Those who carry the red cross of mercy to the front will devoted themselves to the survivors of the machine-gun fire; they will care for the wounded, in order that they can be send back to Death! They will collect money in order to maintain and prolong the conflict.

"They will not know why they are acting thus and will believe they are only doing it out of patriotism. In reality, they will be doing it out of instinct. Woman! The true, saintly Frenchwoman or the enemy woman, will assist Destiny. And she will be decorated for her collaboration. And that will be just, since the only men and women who can perceive the Martian vibrations are of the elect race of the constructors of peoples. Pacifists are degenerates or psychic *agents provocateurs*. No morality, and no religion, can resist the astral influences."

"Well, since you know so many things, can you tell us whether France will be victorious?"

"Yes—but how rude and precarious her victory will be!"

"Will we be able to return to our hearths by Christmas?"

"For several years the new year will see you in uniform."

"What an absurdity! With present weaponry, the war can't last for more than three months, if that!" said the advocate.

"You think so, but the red spiral that has departed from Japan will unfurl its murderous waves over central Europe, pass on to America and pass over us again, bringing the brains of the majority of humankind to the boil. People will kill one another, continuously, for four years, and in an intermediate fashion for fifteen. And the war will be the baptism of blood of a new religion, which will cause even more to flow. For the apostles of every ideal, who have no science, are more ferocious than barbarians."

"Madame, I cannot tolerate your speaking with such disrespect about our sacred convictions!" cried Louis Dubar's father, suddenly. "In sum, you're a fatalist. Fatality caused collapse in Greece and in Islam. I believe in God! He will bless our weapons, and I bow in advance to his will!"

"Yes..." Tussilia smiled, sadly "Your fatality is called God and you are already submissive to it, but the fathers of today are responsible for all the crimes that are about to be committed."

"Us? Murderers? The woman is mad!"

"What did I tell you!" said Madame Montala, triumphantly

"Criminals, certainly. Who has committed the faults that have led to this conflict? Fathers, the sage, the old. Who will expiate those faults? Their sons! Innocents, who have not voted, have not talked irrationally, have not gambled in stocks and shares. The fathers have not been conscious of what they were doing; they are all unfortunates who have been forced to prepare the martyrdom of their sons. The instincts to which they are obedient are those of the antediluvian vivipares. Except that they bear within them so many robust vibrions that the vandalism of a generation counts for nothing in the calculations of their race. You would be murderers, Messieurs, if you could resist the astral, but because you cannot, you are simply worthy of pity."

"Madame," implored Madame Dubar, "since you know so many things, will my son...?" He sentence ended with a sob.

"And mine?" murmured Madame Montala, her hands pressed together.

"Mesdames," said Madame Wiscorney, softly, "I could leave you in anguish, and avenge myself for your wounding insinuations, but the science of Brahma permits me to be generous. Pierre and Louis will come back, one laden with glory, the other with medals—which is not always the same thing. That ought to suffice for you."

"What are you going to do during the torment?" asked Pierre, affectionately

"Keep quiet and play my part in the unusual sacrifices that destiny will demand. I shall share in your astrological delirium, give my fortune and sing the red glory in order not to hear the cries of rage, dolor and hatred that will emerge from millions of young breasts. In spite of the victory, after the epidemic, misery will decimate your fatherland. The golden calf will still be standing, but so emaciated that its feet of clay will be perceptible. Unreason will triumph over wisdom, because we shall all be insane...fit for a straitjacket...for fifteen years. And my soul will be breathless and broken by it...

"In 1926 or 1927 a conjunction of Venus with Mars will lead to brief but violent fratricidal struggles.[29] That will perhaps be the most lamentable phase of the Martian action. Then the influence of the lunar cycles will be felt, and from 1933 onwards, miserable Peace and devastated Progress will know an era of romantic and weary serenity.

"Once it has killed, an animal devours, sings and shakes itself, while the soul dreams or prays.

"Maya and I are going to return to Barbizon. Save for Pierre, I do not want anyone to trouble our retreat. A foreigner and an Initiate, I will perhaps not always be able to keep silent, and I don't have the right to hinder Destiny. It's already too much that I've dared to qualify it this evening. Adieu, then, all of you, for whom I feel great pity."

Tussilia bowed respectfully and left the drawing room with her head held high and her gaze feverish. And while she draped herself gravely in a supple mantle, the relatives and friends whom she had, in turn, exasperated, interested and troubled, looked at one another, astounded.

---

[29] The author might have written this line in 1925, although the novel was not published until 1926, in which case it would be a guess, but it is possible that the Chinese Civil War of 1926 occasioned by Chiang Kai Skek had already broken out, occasioning the remark. She was, of course, far too optimistic in predicting that an era of peace would begin in 1933.

"What if she's telling the truth?" someone thought aloud.

"Evidently, there's something in it," added a neighbor.

"There's devilment underneath it," said a woman.

"Bah! Fundamentally, she's a great intelligence, who has worked on assumptions of which we're unaware and which are perhaps as imaginary as those that are dear to us," concluded Monsieur Montala.

In the meantime, Pierre and Maya were sure of not being mistaken, for they were saying to one another: "I love you! I love you!"

They repeated the three divine words, commenting on them with long pressures, until reality extracted them from their dream.

They were outside the Marquis d'Angeville's house, and the supreme adieu of those three exceptional individuals were simple and dignified, as befit the sacred science of Brahma.

"Always wear the swastika of initiates," said Tulissia, "and call me if you're in danger."

"I shall go with you, but beware of sirens—I'm jealous," said Maya.

"I love you, and I believe," Pierre replied, simply.

The door of the house closed on the two women and the young man, plunging into the darkness, darted his clear gaze at the millions of stars that were scintillating sanctimoniously on high.

"My old Mars," he said, recklessly, "since you hold sway...we're going, we're going!"

And thousands of tiny stars seemed to be winking joyfully.

....

....

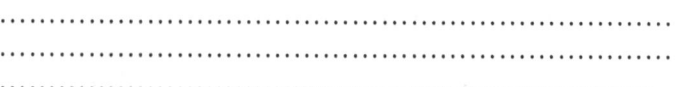

What the war was, from the military viewpoint, there is no point in retracing here. But the distance of time is already sufficient today for the reflex that death produces in hearts to be detachable. The erotic dementia of that epoch attained such unusual paroxysms that a blush rises to the face when one evokes the memory of it.

From pure young women to the exceedingly mature, all the daughters of Eve reveled in unbridled sensuality. Only the death of a loved one rendered a little temporary sanity to the crazed. And even the laments of heartbroken mothers did not impede the interminable song of amour that emerged from every smile, all epistles and all alcoves.

Aging whores with tarnished faces, drunk on the apostolate of the great reinforcement of patriotic literature, even attempted the impossible.

To the offer of a heart, a poilu always replied with the demand for a body, and often a purse as well. Money was sent, and during the leave that followed, the soldier vandalized an ugliness once resigned to purity. And thus were perpetuated odious psychic crimes, for the unfortunates no longer had either pride or virtue to sustain them after the abandonment, nor the dream of an idealized happiness.

The vertigo of the nuptial whirlwind took on a formidable amplitude and velocity. One wrote, was taken, fell pregnant, forgot, laughed, treated all modesties with the same cynicism; and love was never able to slake its hungers in an atmosphere of such base animality. The provinces and the capital, in that regard, entered into a frenzied competition, and if humans had not been attained by the Martian folly, nothing could have explained certain facts.

This one, for example.

It was in 1916, in a village in the Pas-de-Calais, occupied by the Germans. The local grain-alcohol factory and mine had been closed or half-destroyed. The local Maire had rations distributed to all the women and none, young or old, was suffering from starvation.

One day, the Maire in question received twenty of his administratees, who had asked for passes to go to the next village. The worthy man, knowing that enemy troops were about to arrive in that very village, refused them, saying: "You can go in three days."

"Why?"

"Because a regiment of the hussars of death are about to pass through."

"Exactly. That's why we've put on clean underwear."

And it is necessary to emphasize here that those women were not prostitutes.

In all times, fear has produced sexual aberration. The infinitely small entities that our blood carries are maddened by the agitation and terror of souls. Those that can risk the future stage trouble the human brain, male or female, with their impatience, and thus the most sacrilegious acts are accomplished.

When after the war, the women of the above anecdote saw their Maire again, whom ruin and exile had aged to the point of rendering him unrecognizable, several of them dissolved in tears.

"Oh, the Boches! The swine!" they said, in chorus.

"Bah! So you don't change your underwear any more, to go to the Uhlans!"

All of them hung their heads, and one of the murmured: "It's true, all the same, that we lost our heads!"

And the great Frenchman who had spared them a shame smiled and forgave, because, in German prisons, he had had the leisure to meditate on the astral influences that had been explained to him by Annie Besant. He had also learned about the absurd and comical unions that very austere parents had approved. For instance, those of young Frenchwomen between sixteen and eighteen years of age, completely ignorant of English, who were married to American officers or soldiers who did not know a word of French, with all the requisite formalities. The fiancés laughed, and that was sufficient. Those burlesque unions were nothing, in sum, but conjugal prostitution, for, if souls can neither know one another, nor please one another, nothing can justify the procreative act legally. But the common sense of our French bourgeois was as delirious as that of the rest of the nation with regard to the question of "amour."

Thus it is in martial hysteria, as in rabid animals. Not all Frenchwomen succumbed, but all were tempted by the lottery of pleasure.

To begin with, the twins did for their fiancés what all their sisters in anguish did in 1914. First, there were parcels tenderly made up of linen, cakes, tobacco and woolens. Then the letters became increasingly ardent; from weekly, they became daily, and the first epistolary audacities arrived from the front.

Pierre and Maya, having august ideas regarding amour, devoid of literary equivocations and slyly troubling mysteries, resisted the perverse ambience that surrounded them for some time.

Ghislaine and Louis Dubar, prepared for the moral fall by literary and musical suggestions, seconded by the cynicism of one and the ignorance of the other, succumbed in the first few months. That was fatal! After having anesthetized the mind with fervent and seductive words, sent and received, both thought themselves the heroes of a unique and sensational romance.

At the moment when he was about to return to the front, Louis said to Ghislaine: "I'm sure that I won't come back!"

"Louis!"

"And that I shall die without having possessed you…my adored."

"Take me," said the pious child, whose logic had been turned upside down by a thousand tales, in prose or verse, that were running around the salons, the workplaces, the hospitals, and even the sacristies.

The young advocate, who had used his leave to lay siege to General Headquarters, carefully refrained from confessing that he was not going back to the trenches. He collected, with a Mephistophelean smile, the orange-blossom that flowers equally well in romanticism and sincerity. He carried back to the third line the pleasant memory of an ambered Madonna, blushing and modest, whose gaze had lost, under his kisses, the special clarity with which the eyes of virgins are bathed, as if veiled. After the initiation, women's eyes seem to be weeping without tears, mourning the death of the most beautiful of their dreams.

No one around Ghislaine suspected her fault. She did not have the remorse that might have assailed her a year before. On the contrary; as the newspapers, in the form of stories, were recounting the worst derogations of social laws and celebrating the irregular maternities—provided that the seducer had died for the fatherland—Ghislaine thought herself simply admirable. Her young friends were, moreover, making her savorous confidences. All of them had at least two or three godchildren, and each of them tore, to a greater or lesser extent, the veil of the young

Christian vestal. Maya's sister did not consider that she had sinned. On the contrary, were not all weaknesses of the heart filed, in those days, under the rubric of "Service of the Fatherland"?

The poilu knew terrible hours under the shells, but sweet pleasures were reserved for him to equilibrate his nerves between attacks.

....
....

One morning in January 1916, Madame Wiscorney saw the dowager Madame d'Angeville arrive at the Villa Ourton, her expression utterly distressed.

"Madame," said the poor grandmother, so pale that Tussilia felt a great pity for that distress, "I treated you shamefully on the eve of the mobilization, because I thought you infernal or demented. Alas, it's you that were right. We have all gone mad. Even I have allowed myself to be overtaken by the unreason. Like so many others, after having protected Ghislaine from all reality and all ambushes, I have done as all the others have done. I've abandoned the reins, and my little girl has passed without transition from the overly pure bosom of the family to the hospital and work, the cynicism of words and the brutality of things. And now she's lost!"

"Lost? What do you mean?"

"She's dishonored—soiled, you understand? I surprised an argument between her and her fiancé; irreparable words were spoken. Monsieur Dubar no longer desires Ghislaine, who has given herself to him...yes, Madame, given...can you imagine that? A girl so well brought-up, so religious!"

"No confession has ever cut the throat of nature, Madame."

"And when I came in, rage in my heart, I found Ghislaine fainted on the floor of the small drawing room. I hastened to care for her, and it was while undressing her hat the supreme shame was inflicted upon me. When I tried forceful massage to warm up her chilly body, I remained breathless and devoid of thought before the abnormal development of her abdomen. I still doubted the truth, when a slow swell agitated my little girl's right side. At the same moment, the poor girl opened her eyes, and before my horrified expression, she uttered a cry and murmured: 'Forgive me.'

"Forgive! That's easy to say. I can forgive her, but society won't forgive me! And her father even less. If Louis Dubar were at least dead! But he's safe behind the lines, the most decorated man in France!"

"And what does Ghislaine think? What does she intend to do?"

"That's precisely the case of conscience that I've come to submit to you, for I no longer know where my duty lies. Since the man has abandoned Ghislaine, only three outcomes are possible: to live dishonored, splashing with her sin relatives who couldn't do anything about it; to kill herself, which is in conformity with the most scrupulous honor, but contrary to Catholic law; or to kill the child in embryo. For, after all, no Biblical or evangelical text specifically forbids that action, and the Church fathers are not in accord with regard to the moment that the soul enters the body. Perhaps it wouldn't be doing any wrong to anyone if we were to adopt that solution. But as I feel completely confused, I've come to ask your advice. Believe that it costs me a great deal. Your triumph is so humiliating for me! But sure as I was of God, I've been doubting him for two days. How has he permitted such a thing?"

"Don't mix up God with your petty social and family tangles. To resist the attractive force of vehiculated atoms, Madame, only Truth and the radiant force of reason are sufficiently strong."

"I have, however, developed the latter in Ghil, and God..."

"Reason is mutilated by every lie that impacts on the mind of an adolescent. In lunar or hermetic times, there's no danger in playing with amour. The illusions of Agnes[30] are warmed to white heat, and in social calm, arrangements are made in such a fashion that the chosen spouse benefits from that state of the soul. Your fault is as great as hers, so be indulgent and good."

"But her father?"

"I'll take charge of that."

"And the child?"

"I'll take charge of that too."

"Then you're advising me against forced deliverance?"

"With all my energy, and this is why: on the one hand, religion professes great scorn for the body and elevates the soul; on the other, legislators profess a great interest in the body, especially for that of a child; there is forced labor for the abortion and the Caesarian operation for the poorly-constructed mother. What it is necessary to protect, to save, after all, is the child. Why, then, does science not contrive a liaison between civil ideas and religious beliefs? By virtue of willful ignorance! In order to perpetuate the profits of mystery.

"Explain yourself."

---

[30] The reference is to the patron saint of chastity, engaged couples, rape victims and virgins.

"It's so simple that I don't understand your hesitation. If Ghislaine is prevented from giving birth to the animal form that is inside her, she deprives of its means of evolution a soul that is only striving to fulfill its mission with regard to the spirit that animates it. She commits a psychic crime and a social fault. She renders herself culpable toward God, toward nature and toward humans."

"But God has said that the work of the flesh is only desirable in marriage."

"He had been made to say many things that he has never thought."

"And honor?"

"We're talking seriously, are we not? Only the honor of the deserter of amour is stained. Louis Dubar deserves to punished, and Ghislaine to be helped. Send her to me."

"Undoubtedly. But...society? And the young Marquise d'Angeville? What shame? But...since the Gospel is not ashamed of the makers of angels....?"

"Madame, let's leave it at that. Down here, there is Truth and there is human stupidity. A soul is waiting; a body will be born; the priest and the legislator are watching out for you. Remember that it is God himself who activates life. I can't say any more to you."

"Oh! I came to you hoping for I don't know what miracle. You're not even a witch; you don't know of any philter?"

"There are only two: logic and bounty."

"I'll go, then...Ghislaine will be very disappointed. Don't mention her secret to Maya."

"I haven't convinced you? I sense that you're leaning toward the most odious crime."

"I'm going to save the honor of my family."

And the dowager grandmother d'Angeville lowered the violet veil of her hat over her pale and distressed face.

169

A fortnight later, an ambulance deposited a poor little bloodless silhouette at the Villa Ourton, who had to be carried to her bed. It was Ghislaine, who had been disencumbered of her maternity, and brought within an inch of death by a hemorrhage. In order to deceive the malicious gossip of benevolent Parisian society, mention had been made of appendicitis, and there was an accursed hour while the father, grandmother and stepmother waited pitilessly for the result of the criminal operation. About Ghislaine, so pampered until then, no one had cared. Let her die, if God decided thus; never had an Angeville sinned, other than in the arms of a king, and under the protection of a husband with a blazon gilded at the expense of the people. It was impossible to fall from grace!

The father of the twins, it is true, had had the intention to provoke Louis Dubar and inflict upon him the correction that he merited, but he understood very quickly that silence was the only possible scar for the family wound. In any case, it was agreed in that epoch that even the blood of those behind the lines was sacred. The clever ones, like the young advocate, were keeping themselves in reserve for the victory parade.

In the meantime, they calculated that, since men were being killed in millions, the survivors would be at a premium in the marriage market, and some of them went so far as to say: "In 1914 I was worth a hundred thousand francs; now I'm worth five hundred thousand. No one shall have me for less."

Mars lowers the mask of the civilized Kastéhus.

....
....
....
...

Maya wept for a long time at her sister's bedside and received, blushing, the unfortunate child's confidences. It seemed to her that she was entering fully into a world of ferocious larvae, uniquely spurred by the appetites of the senses.

One day, after a sob, Ghislaine had collapsed on her sister's breast, crying: "I'm unhappy, Maya! Save me, for I feel that I still love him."

The young Initiate hugged her to her heart and replied, softly: "Since you despise him, my dear, you can't love him."

"What does his soul matter to me? What I weep for is his caresses, and the sensuality I obtained from them. Can't you save me from this humiliating distress?"

"Perhaps. I'll go ask my Lia."

When Madame Wiscorney returned from the forest, she found Maya in her laboratory, pale and trembling, leaning over a box so old that one could not define, at first glance, where it was made of copper, wood or cardboard. The young woman looked at her with such a hateful expression that the old Hindu was astounded.

"What is it, child? You haven't touched the Pourba, I hope?"[31]

"No, because I don't know how to use it. But since you promised to bequeath it to me one day, I've come to ask you for it."

"In order to do what?"

---

[31] A pourba is a symbolic dagger sometimes employed in Tibetan Buddhism for "letting in light" through bodily chakras

171

"To avenge my sister and punish the guilty party."

"Then you shan't have it yet, my child."

"You refuse to do justice, even though you dispose of immense power?"

"Calm down first; we'll talk later."

But youth does not admit easily that anyone should dare to block its anger. Put in contact for the first time with the evil energies of the Kastéhus, an old instinct caused the young woman to stand up in revolt against the age-old enemy.

"It's necessary that he die, the thief of honor, the deserter of love. And it's me who'll rid society of him."

"No, you won't do anything."

"Give me the secret of the Pourba and you'll see!"

"As you wish—but listen first."

Then, almost as pale as her wimple, Madame Wiscorney opened the ancient box. On a cushion of yellow cloth whose weave was frayed and faded, a delicately slender stiletto appeared, of which it was very difficult to recognize the metal. The light projected glimmers rather than reflections on the barbaric carvings of the hilt. In spite of the humility of its dark and neutral color, the object inspired a terror so intense that Mays recoiled, her heart full of dread and already less enthusiastic to administer justice.

"That is the Pourba, my dear; you can, during a third degree trance, send it to stab someone who has sinned—but remember this well: no one ought to take revenge themselves if they truly desire the punishment of the guilty. As you know, immanent justice is automatic, infallible and merciless. Every gesture inspired by hatred diminishes the severity of the expiation. Know that forgiveness is the cruelest and most implacable of verdicts; it delivers the body and soul of the sinner to all the rigor of magnetic furies."

"Forgiveness can be malevolent?"

"Forgiveness is the withdrawal of the plaint addressed to the Eternal. But, as it releases the thought of the victim, the psychic forces are completely at ease to punish, and their rage is increased by all the confidence and bounty of which the offended party gives proof."

"Is there nothing to do down here then but weep?"

"One can permit oneself a few vague reprisals, but one risks falling into the errors of black magic; it's necessary to use them with prudence. You know the effects of virgin wax; you can exercise your anger without too great a danger to anyone. But forgive instead, forgive! Do you still want the Pourba?"

"No—it scares me."

....
....
....

By dint of seeing Ghislaine weep, however, and becoming indignant at the story of Louis Dubar's dishonest maneuvers, Maya lost all wisdom. One morning, Tussilia surprised her kneading a ball of wax freshly extracted from a beehive. Standing still, she watched her granddaughter's gestures and saw her, fearfully, mold a vaguely human form, press it between her palms and, with al her will-power, summon the aid of the strength of an elemental. She perceived, quite clearly, the advent of the being, simultaneously fluid and brutal, which, as it brushed her, gave her the impression of a hairy body.

When Maya perceived the presence of the one that she wanted to charge with a malevolent mission, she picked up a needle and ran it through the wax figurine.

"You who have been addressed to me by the beyond," she said, "here is a culpable. Study his portrait in my thought, and find the place where he resides. He is a coward lurking behind the lines, but he wears many decorations on his chest. Now, listen…I do not want him to die, but I do not want the cross of the Légion d'honneur ever to put a red stripe on his dolman or his buttonhole. My dearest wish is to see him covered in ridicule and scorn."

"Stop!" cried the old Hindu, trying to make her drop the little mass of wax.

But it was too late. Maya had already—and with what rage!—made the sign of Saturn over the wax. Immediately, something like a rapid flight cut through the air of the laboratory.

"Fool! You've just troubled the serenity of your amour!"

"Pierre has nothing in common with that wretch, my Lia."

"My dear, in teaching you to manipulate dangerous forces, I did not hide any of their reactions, and I warned you against the reflexes of vengeance. You're going to carry out a sad experiment."

....

....

Six months later, a veritable scandal burst forth in the Press. Louis Dubar, put forward as a candidate for the cross of the brave by an obliging minister, suddenly found himself the butt of the sarcasms of his colleagues at the Palais. A popular balladeer made him a target, and, the Chancellery having set aside his candidature ostentatiously, the military authority felt obliged to send him to the front line, in order to permit him to rehabilitate himself.

The day when the news became known at Barbizon, Maya was indiscreetly triumphant. Ghislaine applauded with both hands, but Tussilia, heartbroken, wept hot tears.

"The imprudent girl! Save the poor imprudent girl!" she prayed, with all her heart.

....

....

For a little more than two years, Pierre and Maya escaped the sentimental seism that caused so many customs to collapse and cracked the most solid traditions. But the daily harassment of example, the perfidious counsels of ennui, the realism of trench dialogues and the demands of a young and vigorous flesh eventually eroded the new faith of Infantryman Montala.

One evening, in the month of August 1917, after an agitated stint on the Somme front, he followed his comrades into one of those sad taverns that one often finds in the second line, whose back room is populated by so-called *filles de joie*. The alcohol, the enervation of the danger run and the cerebral paralysis that the proximity of death inflicts on the most valiant, impelled him into impure arms, and caused him to find a measure of softness in the nocturnal kisses of a debased woman, weary and expert at the same time.

When he woke up, he felt so nauseated by what he had done that he was gripped by a mad rage against everything and everyone. Naturally, because he was a man, and young, pride forbade him to confess that he had done wrong, and in any case, guilty parties of his sort never think so. First of all, he incriminated women in general, and his sad companion in particular. Then, thinking that Maya might be unhappy if she knew, his fury knew no bounds.

In a second, he devastated his ideal, and, as the drunkenness of the night before had not entirely worn off, he cried like a man possessed: "Damn it and damn it again! They bore me with their Redeemer, the Brahma, their fluid and their ubiquity!"

"What's that you're saying, dear," said a hoarse voice beside him.

"I'm saying that I've had enough of Them, of you and me!"

"Who's Them?"

"A madwoman and a..." As he was about to profane his love, Pierre hesitated momentarily, but he was in such a state of overexcitement that he emphasized his blasphemy.

"Yes, I repeat, a madwoman and a...schemer."

Scarcely had he doubted his beloved than a great frisson ran through him. An impalpable and glacial air current brushed him, and in the middle of the malodorous chamber in which he had been enfevered, he saw Maya, diaphanous and immaterial, who was contemplating him with amazement, her eyes full of dolorous surprise. He perceived a sort of groan, which had the effect of causing his brutal pride, caught in default, to shiver.

"Well, what?" he said. "Yes, it's me! I'm not made of the wood of which Mages are made, I'm passing the aureole to someone else, damn it!"

The vision vanished at those words, and Pierre, ashamed and desperate, leapt to his feet. The whore watched him get dressed, not daring to say anything. She had seen so many heroes quit her without a word, their lips curled in disgust and their eyes troubled, that she consoled herself for the further affront by saying to herself: "Just another boor. I wouldn't have thought it—he was so polite!"

As soon as he had buckled his tan leather belt, Pierre hung his satchel around his neck and mechanically—because he did it every morning—checked its contents. His pipe, a tin of corned beef, his card-holder, a crust of bread, cartridges, all stuffed in with handkerchiefs and a pair of socks. He put out his hand to open the card-holder, where photographs of Maya and Madame Montala awaited the daily glance and reverie.

No, not here...because of Maman, he thought, because Maya...so much the worst for her. She had only to do as Ghislaine did, and it wouldn't have happened. Ghislaine, there's a woman! That one has a heart and senses...while the other, with the old madwoman, has nothing but nerves. I've had enough of it...enough. How stupid I've been! Word of honor, they'd put a spell on me, the two of them. Oof! I can breathe. What's broken the spell? Perhaps it's this lass.

"Are you part Bohemian, Carmen?" he exclaimed.

"Perhaps so," the whore sniggered.

"I'll come back tonight. I can pay for that."

"If you like," said the pale prostitute, with utter indifference.

Once out of that atmosphere of vice and drunkenness, however, the fresh country air and the gilded light of an August morning soon returned a little of his conscience and lucidity. While his comrades busied themselves with preparations for the next meal, he drew away from their groups and the military barracks. In the distance, the cannons were thundering; one the nearby road, artillery supply-wagons were hastening to replenish the batteries, with a metallic clanking as sinister as the death they were ferrying.

A hundred meters away, a picturesque ruin attracted his attention. The gutted roof had the patina of exceedingly old constructions, and serenity seemed to emanate from its doorway and its latticed windows. Approaching the building, he recognized the remains of a poor and ancient chapel, whose charm and mystery had been violated by a German 120 shell.

He went in. The altar must have been hit during a service, because an embroidered cloth, a paten and a stole were still lying on the ground. The open tabernacle, where no host could any longer be profaned, served as a refuge for a bird's nest. Three stations of the cross were hanging down, in tatters, from sections of wall that were still intact, and insects were buzzing with so much vigor in the penumbra that one might have thought it the murmur of distant nuns chanting matins.

Pierre sat down on the broken baptismal font and meditated. God was impotent to defend his temples, then! He did not protect churches and cathedrals either—and that indifference had already given the Christian slumbering in his soldier's heart pause for thought. God was not, therefore, the enemy of war, since he raised no miraculous protest against it, since he admitted that the purest masterpieces erected to his glory by the piety of men should be burned or destroyed, thus disinteresting himself in his faithful followers and his religion. How quickly peace would be assured, universal and forever, if every homicidal gesture rebounded on the offensive Cain! It would then be indisputable that God does not want hecatombs, and abhors them.

But after three years of war, how could history be reconciled with faith?

In full philosophical flight, Pierre's thought suddenly rediscovered, in the lessons of Brahma and the verities taken from old Tibetan manuscripts, the response to the questions that were crowding his mind. Since the commencement of hostilities, moreover, he had understood the justice of the explanations given by Tussilia, and his courage had received mysterious strength therefrom. And then, had he not lived sublime and sweet hours when the lot had selected him for the listening-post, and he had remained alone and alert during moonless nights devoid of warmth? He had never had to struggle against fear or drowsiness because, after a time, when his eyes struggled to pierce the darkness, he saw something like a swirl of mist advancing toward his observation-port. It made no sound, enveloped him gently, and then recoiled two meters away, either into the tunnel or the beaten earth. By turns, it took on the form of virile or angelic beings. Time had no longer dragged, and no terror had been able to make him shiver. He dreamed.

One evening, in the middle of his watch, he had suddenly seen one of his comrades surge forth in front of him, a cheerful fellow, always joking, who had said to him, putting his hand to his breast: "The plums are indigestible tonight!" And the next day, he had learned that his friend had died at the precise moment of his vision, struck in the heart by a bullet.

Oh, the beautiful things that he had learned in the silence, under soft psychic gazes! He thought, and each of the questions that his mind touched on received a response that amazed his logic. That telepathy of souls plunged him into an ecstasy, which abolished all physical fatigue in his body. Dawn chased the dear phantoms away, and for a long, long time, waiting for the relief or for his comrade on watch to wake up, he commented internally on the truths that had illuminated his life that night.

Once, he had overflowed with such delights that he had dared to tell the doctor that hazard had designated as his duty companion about his adventure. The sawbones had dropped the scalpel that he had been wielding in America in August 1914, and because he liked adventure he had never consented to put on a major's smock. He wanted to go on patrol, to fight, to run all the risks of war and sneer at death.

The doctor listened to Pierre with interest, shook his head, and said: "After all, why not? Wireless telegraphy has revealed the swarming of so many invisible and unknown vibrations, why should thought not have a power identical to that of sound?"

Then, as fear of ridicule weighs upon the intelligences mot open to progress, he added a moment later: "Unless you're simply going mad, ripe for a padded cell!"

A shell bursting close by had almost buried them alive, and the conversation had had no sequel.

The doctor's *why not?* imposed itself, quite simply, on Pierre's semi-somnolent mediation on the debris of the baptismal font, and he felt a vague remorse regarding his blasphemy that morning.

"I believe that I've gone a little over the top," he murmured, in his soldier's vocabulary. "But then, why did she come? Is that any place for a young woman? And then...Louis Dubar's arguments have shaken my convictions. What neither my mother's tenderness nor the objurgations of the chaplain could achieve, that devil's advocate has succeeded in doing. I'm afraid, now, of being the victim of two clever women who are making a fool of me—and that, I won't allow anyone to do. It's this damned Redeemer, above all else, that worries me. For the moment, a good bottle and a lovely girl summarize all my aspirations. And then...I've had enough, of everything...of life of love of everything! In an hour, I might be dead. So? Error or Truth...what does it matter?"

He had scarcely muttered hose words than he saw, floating in front of him in the midst of a red halo, the Swastika of the Initiated.

"Good God of Gods! Are they going to pursue me all day long?" he howled. "Well, Mesdames, you'd do well to give me proof of your science today, for otherwise, I'll never set foot in Barbizon again. You've driven me mad and I've had enough!"

He had risen to his feet in a state of indescribable fury, and he tried to seize the sacred image so dear to lamaists—but his fingers were unable to grip anything, and the impossibility exasperated him to such a degree that he started laughing, the laughter of the crazy or the damned.

"Pay for a drop and it will pass," said a voice nearby.

Then he realized that, in wanting to pursue a vision, he had reached the road, and that comrades were surrounding him, considering him with pitying gazes.

"What do you want? The bug that bit you? She's over there."

And they drew him, laughing, toward the hideous tavern, where he saw Carmen again. Between two glasses of alcohol, he made sure of the girl for the following night, paying her in advance.

All day long, he brooded his bewilderment at being harassed, demoralized and at the end of his tether. In the evening, almost lucid, he was tempted not to go back to the low prostitute, but his masculine pride stifled his nascent remorse.

....
....
....

While that psychic drama was unfolding in a camp on the Somme, the Villa Ourton was abuzz. To begin with, a vague anxiety had woken Maya up that morning, and as, quite naturally, she had feared that it might be a matter of a vibration concerning danger to Pierre, she had taken the sacred Swastika in her hands and put herself in a trance.

To rejoin her fiancé was child's play to her, and the dolorous amazement that gripped her on finding him in a bedroom reeking of wine, musk and lamp-oil, in the company of a creature whose aura was all substance and sensuality, had stopped her heartbeat. When the young man's wounding words had profaned their faith and their love, she had fallen to the floor in a profound faint.

Tussilia had come running immediately, and reanimated her granddaughter by means of prompt and energetic care. She ended up disentangling the cause of Maya's despair.

"He suspects me and he's betrayed me! Horror! And with whom! If you'd seen that woman, my Lia! An elemental, Grandmother. And not even that...a degenerate larva, eaten away by filthy parasites!"

"Calm down, my child, and come and pray at the Chaos of Yama."

....
....

In the rocks, Maya, shaken by sobs, put her face in her hands for a long time, weeping with a dolor too great and too violent for her poor bosom. Finally, appeasement was brought about by the detachment of the poor distressed soul. The body was then able to resume the normal rhythm of animal life. Tussilia, two paces away, stiffened by an extraordinary nervous tension, contemplated her darling and called all the psychical forces at her disposal down upon her head. They came in a host, in a formidable whirlwind. The two women had to hug one another in order not to be knocked down and bruised. They whistled tempestuously, passing close by, oppressing their breath and throwing them against the ricks. Then the agitation stopped and an oppressive silence descended upon the forest.

"I'm waiting! Order of the Council?" said Tussilia, aloud.

And a toneless but clear and implacable voice replied: "The Pourba."

"Is it necessary to kill?" the Initiate asked, fearfully.

"No...to engrave."

"I shall obey!"

Weakly, the two women feel to their knees, and, heads bowed, felt icy currents passing over, which brushed them, impressing them with an impulse to flee.

After a few minutes, the air became warm and perfumed again, free of all magnetic radiation.

"I didn't understand the Master's order," said Maya, then.

"Alas, it will be necessary for you to wield the magic stiletto, and that worries me somewhat. That little dagger, made of seven metals corresponding to the seven planets, benevolent or malevolent, has been tempered in blood, and that confers miraculous virtues on it."

"Whose blood?"

"Not animal blood. Don't worry, for this is the time for the revelation of a truth that, poorly interpreted, has given rise to many crimes. In the same way that a automobile is said to have twenty horsepower without containing a single horse, the 'blood' of learned initiates does not contain a drop of arterial or venous fluid. The magic blood is a solution that has all the properties of human blood and has, in addition, the gift of saturating itself with magnetism. It absorbs it as a sponge swells up with water, or charcoal takes up putrid gases. The composition of that chemical blood is lost, but it will be rediscovered during the next cycle of Hermes. The seven metals tempered in that mixture acquire the faculty of levitation, and they obey the will of whoever possesses the talisman. It's necessary, today, that you use mine, to bring back to you and his Destiny the man whom an elemental fluid has soiled."

"What is it necessary to do?"

"Imagine a phenomenon that can convince Pierre of the force of the Truth we know."

"But I don't want to love Pierre any longer. He's betrayed me—and anyway, he hates me."

"Come on, don't talk like Ghislaine. All that's literature! Pierre loves you, and his treason is a peccadillo."

"A peccadillo! To betray me? Me!"

"You, you! What makes you better than anyone else, from the viewpoint of amour? One good-looking girl is as good as another, and it's unworthy of an initiate to speak so loudly about carnal atoms..."

During the entire journey from Cuvier-Châtillon to the Villa Ourton, Maya was delirious with jealousy, anger and rancor, Tussilia contented herself with shrugging her shoulders at the words she heard. After one last crisis of tears, the young woman finally went into the Hindu's laboratory.

"This," said the grandmother, "is the means of making use of the magic stiletto. For half an hour, you place it over your heart, and then you put yourself in a third-degree trance. You seek out Pierre, and when you've found him, you engrave, with the tip of the pourba, the words or the symbols that appear to you to be most apt to convince your fiancé. Avoid hateful words as well as loving ones; chose in preference words of forgiveness. But I warn you that the effort to be made is considerable, and that one emerges from the ordeal utterly exhausted. Don't forget that you're only a woman, but that you have a mission."

"Oh, my mission..."

"Don't forget, either, that Ichvanmouctas are forbidden to kill. In any case, know that if you disobey, my death will be immediate. I am responsible, before the Forces, for the utilization of the Pourba. But I trust you. Go prepare for the prodigy by prayer and meditation."

....
....
....

Instead of praying and collecting herself, Maya spent long hours talking to her sister. Without explaining to her how she had acquired the certainty of Pierre's treason, the jealous beauty related her dolor to her plaintive twin, still suffering since the abortion.

At first, the two sisters said, in chorus: "Oh, men!"— the cry, a hundred thousand years old, by which the vanquished Awaïs always take heaven as a witness of their misery.

What Tussilia, in all her wisdom, had not been able to awaken in Maya, the absurdity of Ghislaine's words did. Soon, the young woman remembered the why of bodily treasons, and a slight blush rose to her cheeks, at not having resisted the fury of the ancestral Beast, the old Mahana, already mutilated but not yet deprived of a soul.

She confessed her illogic and foolishness, and the lesson that her pride had received paraphrased the lesson of Brahma dolorously. In spite of her fiancé's tenderness, in spite of their paths, she was not indispensable to the escape of the infinitely small; any prey whatsoever satisfied their hatred. It was therefore necessary to see life from above, to strive to dominate events, with the aid of the sacred Science. It was necessary to bring back to true love the spouse chosen by her heart and her Guides; it was necessary to free Pierre's psychic wings, which the elementals were striving to weigh down.

Unfortunately, Ghislaine suddenly interrupted her sister's meditations with literary stupidities.

"If I found Louis with another woman, you know," she said, "I'd kill them both. I'd avenge myself! I'd make them suffer! I'd make the weep. I'd..."

Poor Ghil forgot that she had already encountered the infidel in lewd company, and that she had contented herself with going pale and sobbing.

But malevolent words trouble even the profoundest serenity—to such an extent that after dinner, when Maya shut herself in her room to accomplish the order of the Superior Forces, rancorous tears bathed her face.

Fortunately, Tussilia was praying and watching, for she was aware of the unfortunate reflex of certain words on a young woman's nerves.

....
....
....

Toward midnight, therefore, Maya picked up the Pourba and made a sheath for it with her two hands. Without effort, she succeeded in disengaging herself—which is to say, in isolating the magnetic matter from the cellular matter. To begin with she was frightened to feel the aspirant vigor with which the seven metals saturated themselves with her fluid. It seemed to her that a vampire was drinking all the blood from her arteries; then her heart slowed the rhythm of its movements, and there was nothing within her but bliss and repose.

That state only lasted a few minutes, however; suddenly, her will, as if liberated from a great weight, was gripped by an irresistible thirst for action.

The moment has come, let us obey! the extracted soul seemed to be saying. And, with a sensation of horizontal flight, Maya sensed that she was carried northwards. A few seconds sufficed for the subconscious that dominated her to get its bearings. Suddenly, she rejoined Pierre, and, as she had that same morning, she found him back in the sordid room, beside the whore, whose breath had the reek of a wine-cask.

Anger abruptly troubled the serenity of her hypnosis, and without hesitation, because Pierre had his hand on the prostitute's breast, she directed the tip of the Pourba toward that soft and withered breast.

"You must not kill," murmured a voice in her ear.

Then, with a little curt thrust, she drew away the hand of the gallant, who sat up straight—not without alarm!—next to the girl, who croaked: "What are you doing, darling? You're burning me! Mercy! Mercy!"

And as Pierre, leaning over the bare-chested unfortunate, saw a dagger designed over the skin, the point directed at the heart, an invincible fear invaded him. A tremor agitated her lips with so much force that he could scarcely articulate: "Have pity on her! Pity! I believe! I believe!"

Immediately, however, an intense pain burned his own chest, and he fell back on to the pillow, vanquished, while the woman, whose arms seemed paralyzed, wept with little hiccups.

The young man's suffering lasted less than two minutes, and when he was finally able to raise himself up to discover the source of the pain that had lacerated his torso, he saw engraved upon his breast the image of a swastika, and above it, the word *Maya*.

He got up hastily, got dressed, and, his head bowed, left the room without even looking at the prostitute, who, her breast still marked by the red stiletto of the Lamas' instrument of justice, was plunged in a kind of lethargy. Like a madman he plunged into the night, and the dawn found him on a heap of stones, his face bathed in tears, repeating untiringly: "Maya, I love you and I believe! Your faith will me mine! Forgive me!"

....

....

As soon as the offices of his company were open, he asked to speak to the captain, and had a brief and decisive conversation with him. The officer shook the young poilu's hand very vigorously, and a week later. Pierre Montala entered the Le Bourget aviation camp as a train-ee.

This is what he wrote to his fiancée:

I can no longer resist our destiny. I am about to conquer the wings that my mission demands.

When that letter reached Barbizon, there was celebration at the Villa Ourton.

"He's saved," said Tussilia.

"He loves me!" Maya exclaimed. "Oh, my Lia, my Lia, how happy I am!"

"Pooh! The paltry Mahatma, whose first thought is for the joys of this world!"

"But Grandmother, God didn't create life for its sweetness not to be savored."

"You're right, child. Pick all the flowers of youth— but don't forget those of science. Be on you guard."

"Help me, Grandmother."

"Yes, but Pierre's salvation depends on the flexibility of your fluidic emanations. Resume the daily exercises of an initiate, my child."

From that day onwards, the Crazy Rock recommenced its escapades in the forest of Fontainebleau, setting the teeth of hunters and poachers on edge.

....
....
....

Before effecting the definitive flight that would qualify him as a pilot, Pierre Montala came to make honorable amends at the feet of the svelte and troubling Maya. The moral proofs that she had undergone seemed to him to have modeled a graver and nobler visage, and her beauty had been enhanced by an even more captivating charm.

Tussilia allowed them to walk alone in the forest, sure henceforth that the material had been vanquished by the ideal. Perhaps she gave a little too much credit to youth and desire, and if kisses are the vampires of souls, the fiancés must have done a good deal of harm to their respective auras, but the result was not disastrous; the young people played out eternal scenes of love, reproaching the coldness or ardor of their temperaments. Classically, they wept soft tears, and forgiveness died in so many kisses, long, tender or hectic, that they truly had no great merit as sublime beings.

A month later, Pierre was sent to the front to fill a gap left in Escadrille des Cigognes by the death of one of its pilots.[32]

....
....

---

[32] The Escadrille des Cigognes ["the stork squadron"], or combat group number 12, was a famous unit in the Great War, from which many of the most famous figures in French aviation emerged, and whose members played a major role in perfecting what became the standard tactics of aerial combat.

Christmas 1917, it will be remembered, was the most anguished of all the Christmases of the bloody years. Civilians and soldiers alike were exhausted, Europe entire clenched its teeth, and the patriotism of the belligerents was at the end of its tether. Nevertheless, the rictus of laughter was on all faces, in the trenches, in the restaurants and in the taverns. Only the aviators, notably in the Ardennes, paid less heed to the champagne bubbling in their glasses than to the distant throb of Fokkers. As midnight chimed in the poorest churches of France, the alert signal resounded in the camp of the Cigognes. All the lights went out as if by enchantment, and it would have been necessary to witness the departure of the fighter aircraft, in pitch darkness, to comprehend the sinister atmosphere in which the handsome young heroes launched themselves into combat.

Pierre Montala, whose cockpit bore as a fetish not the fashionable doll but the symbol of the Initiates, was one of the first to take to the air and disappear into the silvery veil of the winter night. He had, as a supreme talisman, a silk stocking that Maya had worn—for in that epoch, no aviator risked himself in the clouds if he did not have the illusion of being accompanied by a lovely female leg. The silk stocking sufficed, it appears, to create the mirage.

The aerial battle immediately attained an unusual violence. Three tragic torches striped the darkness: two Cigognes and a Fokker had been shot down, and three human beings had conquered glory in the horror of a furnace. Up above, three enemy aircraft were soon circling the valiant Montala, who was nicknamed "the Phoenix" because he had emerged, thus far, from the continuous fire of machine-guns and bombs without a scratch. He only had two more aircraft to shoot down in order to be proclaimed an ace.

When he saw the three steel hawks menacing his wings, Pierre smiled and murmured: "This evening I'm going to earn my last stripe; that'll be three dinners and twenty bottles of champagne. Let's go, Maya—the first one's yours."

He had said that mechanically, without suspecting that the mere mention of his fiancée's name sent a telepathic wave to Barbizon warning of danger.

At that precise moment, in fact, the young woman woke up, and ran into her grandmother's bedroom like a madwoman.

"Pierre! Pierre! Help me, Grandmother, help me!"

"Kacyapa!" said the Hindu. "To me, Kacyapa!"

Both of them knelt down with their arms crossed, in accordance with the sacred rite, and one might have thought the two statues of wax, on which the red light of the flickering flame of a nightlight was dancing.

With the precise aim that he owed to his father's lessons, the younger Montala succeeded in killing one of the enemy pilots with a bullet in the head, and the aircraft, henceforth devoid of command, descended lugubriously toward the ground, spiraling like a dead leaf.

"And one!" sang the victor, while observing the two Albatroses that were tightening their circuits round him. "Which shall I choose, Maya?"

Ten times he escaped the collaborative efforts of his enemies, and then a fortunate bomb burst the fuel tank of one of his adversaries. He did not have time to rejoice in the vertical fall of the vanquished, for a hail of bullets immediately reached the vital organs of his own apparatus. He sensed that he could no longer veer to the right, no longer being master of his direction.

"I'm f   ," he groaned, and added, sniggering: "It's gone wrong, Maya."

At the same instant, with a superhuman energy, he performed the craziest maneuvers.

I'm insane! he thought, in a moment of lucidity. *I'm committing suicide!*

He no longer had the leisure to comprehend or react, however. The enemy, disconcerted at first, missed two attacks, but succeeded in a third, and then there was the fall, his hands clutching the stick, his eyes closed and respiration impossible...a great noise of splintering woods...and then silence...and an impression of suspension, of air penetrating his intact lungs deliciously.

I must be dead, Montala thought. *It's not disagreeable, I'm swinging, being caressed, it's soft, it's cool...ow! My arm hurts. Ow! I can't open my hand any more. That's because I'm not dead, but I'm wounded! Oof! I can't do any more!*

And without seeking any longer to understand, he lost consciousness of everything.

At dawn, peasants passing through the forest saw, between two trees with ravaged crowns, suspended three meters from the ground, an airplane in whose cockpit an exhausted aviator was fast asleep.

When, with a considerable reinforcement of backbones and ropes, they contrived to reach Pierre, they perceived that he had a dislocated shoulder, three dislocated fingers, and a bruise on his forehead.

"It's a miracle!" the witnesses all cried, in chorus.

"You could say so," said Pierre, extracting the fetish from the debris of his plane. "And I'll thank my talisman for that. But...I think...I've got the blessed wound!"

In the argot of the poilus, that signified at the time: "I'm in for three months of rest, tender care, spoiling and blow-outs."

During the war, the forest of Fontainebleau served as a refuge for all the wild boars that the soldiers and the shells expelled from the thickets of the Ardennes and the Vosges. Those frightful beasts have the ability to run without stopping for hours on end, covering considerable distances overnight. Hunters are quite familiar with the ambulatory mania of that prey, so the old Nimrods who made Barbizon their rendezvous for hunting were very aggrieved by the prefectorial restrictions. And the "good shots" tugged their gray or white beards angrily. To console themselves, they went out in pairs, and carefully examined the imprints left by the animals in the soil. With the gravity of augurs, the most expert affirmed, merely by examining the tracks that the best was so many years old, weighed so many kilos, and that it fur was brown or russet. The timid were open-mouthed with admiration before the sagacity of the smooth talkers.

Robert Dunant often joined his friends and contravened the police regulations after his fashion. His taste for the forbidden game was so keen that he courageously reiterated the exploits of the great hunters of the Renaissance. He went after the boars with a knife, and that method haloed his reputation as a hunter with a very special glory. People were proud to plunge into the forest with him— and his dagger gave his chosen companion a security that was not to be disdained.

On the twenty-fifth of December 1917, Monsieur Montala senior had woken up the indefatigable hunter of solitary boar at daybreak, and both of them, shivering and smoking, lost themselves in the mist of the winter morning.

For a long time they walked in silence, for they delighted in taciturnity, and were each respectful of the other's reverie. When a distant angelus troubled the two friends' meditation, however, Robert Dunant checked the bowl of his pipe.

"Damn! I keep drawing, but there's nothing left inside," he said. "Damnable war tobacco—it's bad and expensive."

"Yes, yes—but I've let Joséphine go out too. What the devil was I thinking?"

"About the same thing as me—the silent gray silhouette that appeared between two rocks a little while ago."

"You saw it too? I thought I was the victim of an illusion. One might have thought that it was a woman, no?"

"Yes, but a woman devoid of arms or legs, a sort of ambulant mummy."

"And rapid, because it disappeared as if by enchantment."

"It was phantom of the mist, a play of the light in the fog."

"Perhaps, but a few meters from there, I thought I heard a sob."

"Really! It seemed to me that I could hear chanting."

"That's scarcely similar. You can see that we've been duped by our senses. There's no one in the Chaos of Yama, because women, thank God, are wiser than men—they're afraid of wild boars."

"Not all of them. Madame Wiscorney, for example..."

"I can no longer talk about her except with deference, since your son Pierre is marrying that enigmatic person's granddaughter."

"Very troubling, that enigma!"

"You'll permit me to laugh, won't you? What's so extraordinary about the old lady? After all, liking the fresh air excessively doesn't make someone a witch."

"You're right, but..."

"Well, then, ask her to bring about my conversion by accomplishing some fine feat of white magic! I say white because it appears that the black is very dangerous. A light?"

"Thanks. Your poilu's lighter is nice."

The two walkers carried on straight ahead, but after a minute' silence, Monsieur Montala said: "All the same, you can't say that my son's a poltroon, can you? Well, I've seen him very troubled by certain phenomena, and I myself..."

"To believe, it's necessary for me to see and touch. I'm of the family of..."

A stone that had tumbled down from a small hillock cut the dialogue short. They both shivered with the same anxiety, exploring the reduced circle of their horizon with their eyes. The thick mist hindered their inspection.

"I think I can hear footsteps...."

"No, it's another stone rolling...in order not to gather any moss..."

"I can assure you, my dear, that I can sense a human presence...it's like a malaise..."

"Personally, I can only sense the wind. Come on, Montala, we've been dreaming too much about marvelous impossibilities."

Robert Dunant's mocking and mordant voice was still vibrating when a breathless form surged forth between two sandstone blocks, pale and yet joyful.

"He's safe!" cried the apparition, throwing her arms around Monsieur Montala's neck. "We've saved him! My poor Pierre!"

"What's happened to my son?" murmured the young man's father, almost ready to faint.

"He crashed last night, in combat. His apparatus is destroyed but he's alive! He's alive!"

"How do you know that already, Mademoiselle?" interrupted Robert Dunant, who had recognized Maya and was trying to catch her in default.

"Because we...we manipulated the forces..."

"What forces?"

"The sparse energies that can be condensed by prayer and put into action by will."

"At what time did Monsieur Pierre crash?"

"About half past midnight."

"And how long have you been in the forest?"

"We left the Villa Ourton at five o'clock.

"Damn! You haven't slept much. Would you think it indiscreet of me to ask the objective of your excursion?"

"It was necessary to thank the Forces as soon as possible."

"Hmm! All this is rather obscure. We'll verify it, with your permission, Mademoiselle."

"As you please, Monsieur."

Then having impulsively kissed her future father-in-law on both cheeks, Maya fled, leaping from rock to rock, occasionally turning round to shout: "He's alive! I'm so happy! I'm so happy!"

Left alone, the two men looked at one another, one laughing disconcertedly, the other very pale, seemingly incapable of a word or gesture.

"Come on, my friend—you're not going to believe in a mishap, when a pretty mouth has just reassured you."

"My son! My son!" howled Monsieur Montala suddenly. "I want to know. I want to know. Pierre! My little Pierre!"

And the worthy man, without paying any heed to his companion, started running in the direction of Barbizon. He went rapidly, his breathing hoarse and his heart oppressed. From time to time he paused, stammering inconsequentially and weeping large tears. Respectful of his paternal anguish, Robert Dunant followed his friend without daring to make a sound. Sometimes, he permitted himself to guide him gently when, at the junction of two paths, he hesitated over the route to take. Finally, the orange trellis of the Hôtel de la Fôret came into view at the end of the Chemin des Mazettes. Only then did the skeptic murmur: "This is the moment to convert me, my friend. It's eight o'clock—the telephone and the telegraph are about to open. Let's seek information."

"That's true! I'm mad! If something's happened, they'll have sent word to Auteuil."

However, the public services were not accessible to everyone. It required an official authorization, with signatures.

"We'll find out more quickly if we take an auto and go to get information from the Ministry."

....

....

It was midday when the poor father, at his wits' end, got home. His mind was in turmoil. He knew that Cigogne no. 4 had not returned to its hangar; that was all that anyone had been able to tell him. He had already climbed half way up the stairs when the concierge stopped him.

"Monsieur? Here's a telegram. I wouldn't let the telegraphist take it up—Madame is so nervous. It might be bad news!"

"Give it to me," said Robert Dunant, imperiously. He had not quit his friend. "I'll open it, shall I?"

There was a ten-second silence, and then a cry of joy.

"*Miraculously saved. One foot burned, one wing dislocated. See you soon. Kisses. Pierre.*"

"What did I tell you!" said Montala, immediately triumphant. "Well, dare you doubt now. What women, my dear!"

"Pooh! Let's not get carried away. Simple coincidence."

"Oh!

"Don't get upset. Let's wait. Anyway, what am I doing here, since you're all right now? I'll go home. *Au revoir*, and a good pipe!

. . . .

. . . .

When Aviator Montala, his shoulder in plaster and his hand bandaged, received his mother's visit at the Val de Grâce hospital, he told her the marvelous story of his adventure and concluded: "It was a pure miracle, Maman."

"Of course," said the poor woman, emotionally. "God owed me that! I'd prayed so much for you!"

Monsieur Montala, who was tugging his moustache nervously, could not help smiling. "Women are decidedly keen to save men by means of mysterious interventions. Can you imagine that Maya also claims…"

"I know," said the invalid, immediately. "I owe her my life, quite simply…"

"What! And God?" cried the indignant devotee.

"God made the forces of which she made use, Mother dear."

. . . .

. . . .

As soon as the injured man was well enough to be sent back to the front, he requested, with the moist respectful firmness, to marry Maya before confronting peril again. His officers and his parents acquiesced to that desire.

As Ghislaine had been truly loved for three months by a young engineer devoid of a fortune, Madame Wiscorney financed him secretly, and the engagement son became official. The marriages of the two sisters took place on the same day, and the smiling crowd applauded their beauty.

It was a very touching ceremony, which took place in the picturesque chapel of Barbizon, which does not resemble any village church, because the École de Barbizon owed God the homage of a studio. Théodore Rousseau, who had two of them, put the larger one at the disposal of the Catholic religion. He was the one who designed the original bell-tower, which harmonized so well with the slightly rustic elegance of the church, and nature strove, every spring, to veil the profane origins of the temple by covering it with a mantle of virgin vines, wisteria and clematis. Mauve petals fell from the florid porch on to the white dresses of the twins, and the dowager Madame d'Angeville wept soft tears.

The father of the lovely brides made a toast at the end of the nuptial meal, in which he affirmed, as nobly as could be, that everything works itself out down here and that the designs of God are impenetrable. He thanked the two educative grandmothers with the same words, but had to turn his head away under the gaze of the old Hindu.

....

....

When Pierre Montala rejoined the Cigognes he was so radiant with confidence and serenity that his comrades congratulated him.

"You're an ace who'll cut all four in the pack," they said, between two glasses of champagne.

That same evening, he recommenced the series of his exploits, which have remained legendary in the annals of the great Escadrille. In August 1918 he received the Légion d'honneur, on the same day that he received a letter which read:

The Redeemer, or his great-grandfather, quivered this morning. The little ogre made me weep with joy. What shall we call him?

Your dear
Maya

....
....
....
....
....

On the fifteenth of February 1919 a pale winter sun was rising slowly over the forest of Fontainebleau when the throb of a powerful engine troubled the calm and pleasant serenity of the Angelus. Flying over the Église de Chailly, whose silhouette was immortalized by Millet, the shortest and stoutest warplane to emerge from the Farman workshops traced an expert parabola in the air, headed straight toward Barbizon and settled, shaken by long tremors, in a field that was still entirely covered in white frost.

Pierre leapt from the cockpit and ran at full tilt toward the Villa Ourton. A telegram had informed him that Madame Montala, against the will of the young household, was bringing a priest of her acquaintance that day to baptize the newborn.

It was in the simultaneously sinister and picturesque costume of aviators in flight that the young husband leaned over his son's cradle for the first time. He took the baby in his arms, lifted him piously above his head like an officiant elevating the host, and kissed him on the eyes and the forehead.

"Precursor or Messiah, you're my kid before all else," he said, laughing, to stave off the emotion that as overwhelming him. "So Maya doesn't want to you be baptized? That won't prevent the Christ from filling the world with his glory and annihilating two civilizations."

"But my dear, Paul wouldn't come to any harm if his soul had received the forces of four elements beforehand. Water alone isn't magic, as you know," replied the young mother.

"What do you say, Maman Tussilia? What should I do?"

"Meditate for a moment, my son, and inspiration will come to you," said the Hindu.

While the great-grandmother cradled the baby, Pierre embraced Maya, and savored her lips. Their eyes penetrated one another, and the ace of aces suddenly exclaimed: "I've found the solution in my wife's gaze. Wrap the kid up tightly, Mother-in-law, prepare a bowl of warm water, and thick veils for the face."

"What are you going to do?" asked the mother, anxiously

"Let the Forces act," the Initiate put in. She shielded the delicate and charming body of little Paul against the north wind personally. At a sign from Paul she followed him, holding a heap of warm woolens in her arm, in which the Predestined of the Prophecies was sleeping.

On seeing the apparatus toward which Pierre was taking her, Tussilia understood what was about to happen. Having set the propeller in motion, the ace of aces climbed into his cockpit, held out his arms and said:

"Send up the Innocent"

"You're right, my son, light is the very soul of fire, and the water of the clouds is purer than that of our wells. Om and Kacyapa are with you!"

Upright and rigid in the middle of the field, Madame Wiscorney watched the monstrous bumble-bee rise into the azure, soon becoming a brown cross outlined against the blue of the Zenith.

"A cross!" she murmured. "The Messiah of tomorrow might perhaps die on a similar cross, but before then, he'll have deposited on earth the Son of Heaven, awaited by the beings in need of redemption."

Pierre circled for a long time up above, flying over immaculate cumulus clouds. The dead religions that all placed their gods in a chariot racing over the clouds returned to his memory, and he understood that other civilizations had solved the problem of heavier-than-air flight. He foresaw, with certainty, that new verities would emerge fatally from the violated Ether, and Madame Wiscorney's prophecies did not appear to him to be at all unrealizable.

He remembered that the larvae of *Meloe* could travel in the fleece of one bee to another apiary if they had the good fortune to be brushed by a dandelion seed drifting in the air. The winged seed detaches them from the golden fly and the wind brings plant and animal alike to rest on another flower where another insect is gathering pollen.

Those insects were sometimes so distant from one another, proportionally speaking, as two planets in a solar system. Aircraft could do for the human larva what the anemone of Savoy and the dandelion does for the *Meloe*.

At that moment, everything seemed possible, and his soul overflowed with a prescience so infinite that a great surge of confidence and faith uplifted him. Veering to face the east, he picked up his little Paul in both hands and offered him to the rays of the winter sun.

"Bathe my son in the gold of your light," he said, fervently, "and may your mystery one day be revealed."

He descended again toward the clouds, and allowed himself a momentary illusion of playing a pagan Apollo. And during the lived dream, the obsession dear to Miarka possessed him.[33] Involuntarily, he cradled his infant to the rhythm of the song of the vagabonds:

"Clouds, how good you are! Clouds, how beautiful you are!

"And my dreams will sleep upon you!"

....
....
....
....
....

Two minutes later, Tussilia, still motionless in the field, saw the steel bumble-bee that bore so much hope and so much fragility descending in broad spirals. Without any shock or jolts, Pierre landed, and handed the child to his great-grandmother.

---

[33] The reference is to the heroine of Jean Richepin's novel *Miarka, la file à l'ourse* (1883), which was adapted for the stage and filmed. The lines of the song that follows are taken from that book; they are not sequential, the first two phrases being the first line and the other the last.

"He has received the baptism of air, water and fire," he said.

"Here is that of earth," said the great-grandmother, taking a little humus and flattening it gently on the baby's forehead.

"But it isn't Ash Wednesday!" joked the father,

"You don't know, then, that the Lenten ceremony is the adaptation of a Saturnian rite that marked the end of ancient celebratory feasts? I've traced the sign of the nebulas on Paul's forehead."

"And now that you're satisfied, Mother-in-law, no history, eh? Let my mother do as she pleases. I want peace in my family, for I need serenity. Do you know that your predictions are coming true? I shall become the king of the air and the bird of tempests."

....

....

The sound of a propeller, a great cold fluid eddy, and Pierre was no longer anything but a streak, and then a black dot in the azure.

Tussilia took little Paul back to the Villa Ourton. He was sucking his thumb like a very hungry predestined one.

After lunch, which brought together Madame Montala, the curé of Chailly, Père Joseph, Madame Wiscorney and Ghislaine, they proceeded very decently with the baptism.

Maya, although plaintive and still hurt, could not suppress an enigmatic smile. It was so profane that the Jesuit asked her the reason for it after the ceremony.

"It's true," she said, "that I had a desire to laugh, for you reminded me of all the enchantresses and magicians who once leaned over newborns to cast spells on them. Nothing was lacking my little darling, for the prayer is an incantation and the saints pure spirits. You summoned them, exactly as spiritualists summon their familiar spirits. Why, then do you pursue the latter with the worst anathemas, since...."

"Don't take the trouble to reply to her," Madame Montala interrupted. "I've told you, she's a witch."

"Oh, that ugly word! Madame is a charming heretic, that's all," the Jesuit concluded, diplomatically.

....
....
....
....
....

Six months after the war, Pierre Montala entered the service of a major airplane manufacturer, in the capacity of a champion racer, and set about breaking all the records; his prowess impassioned the Press and public opinion. That did not prevent him, however, from savoring the joys of the hearth and proving his love of family life by giving little Paul a sister, Gisèle, who was born in the spring of 1920, and then a brother, René, who came into the world in July 1923.

On the day when the younger son's eyes lit up with the divine clarity which is known as "the gaze," Tussilia knelt beside his crib and remained in a trance for more than an hour. Large tears ran from her admirable mask of a Hindu priestess, which one of her admirers had justly described as "a face of old ivory with a patina of burnished gold." An immense dolor twisted her mouth, ordinarily so amiable, albeit grave. And her gleaming eyes, the eyes that had the privilege of perceiving the translucent beings that populate the atmosphere and willingly float into our dwellings, no longer had any but the human softness of ancestors without science, but molded by bounty.

Maya, coming in unexpectedly during that psychic crisis, could not help going pale. For the serenity of her grandmother to have been subjected to such a proof, it was necessary that the superior Forces must have imposed some great duty on her. Not wanting Tussilia to suffer having her disciple witness such a moment of weakness, Maya withdrew discreetly, and waited for Madame Wiscorney to come out of the room.

"What's happened?" she asked, then.

The Initiate, her forehead moist and her hands trembling, could not articulate a sound; she simply opened her arms. For a long moment, the two women wept together; then Tussilia found sufficient calm to say:

"Time has revolved, my dear. The Sage is going to die, and he has designated me to receive, with his last sigh, the isolating and homicidal wax, the animal light, also known as the elixir of life. Every guardian of the Three Supreme Vaults has the right to one drop of that elixir per cycle. Only fifteen remain. Know, Maya, that every drop prolongs existence for thirty-three years, and that I must, therefore, remain on earth for nearly two centuries.[34] Humanity will then have rediscovered the three sacred secrets. I shall launch them into space by means of magnetic vibrations, and I hope that one of our descendants will receive at least one of them. The Sage is waiting for me."

"You've never mentioned this Sage, my Lia!"

---

[34] Unless it is a mistake, the reference to "nearly two centuries" implies—given that fifteen times thirty-three is nearly five hundred, which corresponds with the figure earlier cited as the interval before the impending cataclysm—that Tussilia is due to be replaced as the Sage before the full interval elapses.

"He lives in a cave in the heart of the glacial region. Three months before quitting his carnal envelope, he launches a telepathic message assigning to its recipient a day, and hour and a place of rendezvous. I cannot shirk the order given."

"Grandmother! Don't leave us!" Maya moaned.

"Don't increase my grief, child. Science was sweet in my youth. The bitterness of my life as a wife was palliated by the smile of motherhood. But Paul, Gisèle and René have woven around my soul a web of adorable threads impregnated with tenderness. I had almost forgotten that the hour of mutation would sound today. The magnetism that their plump little arms and silky heads emanate had anesthetized the vigilance of my subconscious. I must go, and I beg you to telephone Pierre to come as soon as possible, for he alone can accomplish the necessary miracle."

"What miracle?"

"It's necessary for me to be on the plateau of Sakia in the Himalaya massif, at an altitude of five thousand meters, in two months and eight days. He will transport me."

....
....

The ace of aces hastened to the Initiate's appeal, and listened to her without saying a word. After a brief silence, he simply declared: "That's good. I was hesitating over an attempt on the Asian record. I'll sign up tomorrow."

"You will be victorious, my son, for nothing can prevent the Sages from coming together at the supreme moment."

....
....
....
....
....

And the day came when Madame Wiscorney plunged for the last time into the forest of Fontainebleau. She stood in front of the Absorbed Rock, and, looking directly into the eyes of the stone mask incrusted in the rock, she murmured:

"Be patient, Brahymus, proud foster-brother of the divine Brahyma; the cataclysm that ought to deliver you and put an end to the punishment that you are suffering is nigh. The Earth is stirring, its cocoon is growing, without humans perceiving it, for the continent of tomorrow has risen by several kilometers without the equilibrium of the tides being troubled thereby. Soon, it will be possible to calculate the enormous quantity of plasma absorbed by the Saturnian larva. Without that absorption of millions and millions of tons of liquid, America and Europe would already be submerged. Patience! Only two and a half centuries separate you from your liberation.[35] Do not harbor any more hatred for me, whose carnal envelope the snows will preserve intact, when my spirit will be far away in the astral. I salute you, O imprisoned force; be kind to those I love and those who demand of your gaze the mystery of your torment. Adieu!"

....
....

---

[35] In view of the figures of "nearly two centuries" and fifteen times thirty-three cited in the previous section, this figure is distinctly odd—as is the sudden introduction of the name Brahymus for the entity previously named as Brahytina, and the revelation that it is the "foster-brother" of "the divine Brahyma." At least one of the three names, and at least one of the three numbers, might be the result of transcription errors, but the passage remains deeply enigmatic nevertheless.

As Tussilia did not take away anything except the magic Pourba and a few manuscripts, and as the kisses she put on the cheeks of her great-grandchildren, were scarcely any longer or more tender than usual, no one apart from her granddaughter and Pierre had any suspicion of her departure. Only Maya, very pale, accompanied her grandmother through the fields. The farm laborers, having finished their hard labor, were going home along the roads and alleyways. They were so tired that they scarcely turned round to watch a robust buzzing airplane land.

"Another one broken down! Why don't they do as we do and stay on the cowshed floor? In my day, we weren't idlers and we didn't go capering around in the clouds! Those dandies need females to occupy them—that's clear their heads."

And with that last observation, which summarized the scorn of the men of the earth, and also the hostile neutrality with which they always paralyze progress, the peasants continued on their way, without looking back.

....
....
....
....
....
....

The newspapers followed, with all the interest it merited, the audacious aerial journey undertaken by Pierre Montala. Dispatches arrived regularly, from every port of all. And then suddenly, the entire European public thought there had been an accident. For forty-eight hours. No one knew what had become of the glorious airplane.

On the indications of Tussilia, it had abruptly changed direction, and then landed on an immense deserted snow-covered plateau.

The north wind stung their faces, and involuntarily, Pierre exclaimed: "Oh, Grandmother, I can't permit you to get out here. It would seem like committing murder. Leave you here? Never! You'd be dead within an hour."

But the Hindu, without replying, detached herself from the uncomfortable seat in which she had remained hidden throughout the journey.

"Have no fear, my son," she said. "Destiny is being accomplished."

A great whirlwind nearly carried the travelers and the airplane away then. Without a kiss, but with a long tender gaze, the old Hindu took her leave of Pierre, who was petrified with horror, his throat full of sobs.

"Maman! Maman!" he shouted, as Tussilia, upright, holding her head high, drew away at a confident stride into the icy immensity.

But the old Hindu did not turn back. She went straight ahead, her arms extended. She went on…and her pace did not slow down. On the contrary, the further she went, the more elastic her stride seemed.

At the idea that an atrocious death awaited that admirable woman, Pierre could not make up his mind to depart. In the end, however, given the futility of his appeals and the necessity of resuming his flight toward Courba before the ice had immobilized his engine definitively, he prepared himself slowly, his soul torn, to resume his pilot's seat.

Then he saw the silhouette of a man surge forth from the depths of the plateau, so emaciated that he could easily have imagine him a skeleton. He floated rather than walked, and hastened toward Tussilia.

Ah! thought the ace. *I can breathe; she's no longer alone! But how can human beings live in the icy hell?*

He was about to start the propeller in motion, but what he saw next paralyzed his gesture, and dazzled him, while overwhelming him with terror.

First of all, the Sage and the Hindu bowed to one another with a kind of respectful piety, while the snow swirled around them to a height of six feet, as if familiar but invisible beasts were plying around them. An accolade held the man and the woman in a momentary embrace, and then the Hindu, alone and with a queenly stride, went into a cavern whose entrance, fringed with frost, became iridescent in the glare of the setting sun.

The sun darted its most powerful ocher red rays eastwards, as if it were conscious of illuminating an apotheosis. And while the Sage marched toward the light at an unsteady pace, arms extended as if in a supreme appeal, Forces raced over the plateau. In an irresistible whirlwind they shifted the plane, and pressed Pierre against his cockpit.—but that crushing only lasted for a few seconds, and the younger Montala was able to breathe easy while the elementals surrounded the old man.

By means of a precipitate rotation they lifted the snow around him, drove it, heaped it up and obliged it to form a kind of pedestal, which bore a strong resemblance to clouds stacked one atop another. Perhaps without him being aware of it, the Sage, immobilized in ecstasy, found himself standing on that dream-platform. Continuing their sacred efforts, the invisibles had son modeled a dazzling and icy throne for him, on to which a second of physical weakness caused the ascetic Brahmin to fall. Facing the sun, and with a slight swinging movement, the platform, the throne and the blessed individual were lifted from the ground to a height of some three meters.

The Sage's visage radiated an intense light, and no adjective could qualify the bliss of his smile.

Pierre saw then, very distinctly, streaks of opaline light separate from his inferior limbs, curve back upon themselves and meet up with the ends of mauve filaments that were abandoning the torso and the arms. The whole condensed into a kind of translucent ball, which veiled the face of the dying man momentarily. Then the ball was detached from the man, and rose into the sky, where Pierre's eyes could not distinguish it for long, because it was as diaphanous and tenuous as a soap bubble.

In any case, the aviator was solicited by another astonishment. Having searched the Sage with his gaze, he understood, from the pose of the poor collapsed body and the lamentably gaping mouth, that there was no longer anything there on the throne of snow but a cadaver like all other cadavers. This one, however, by virtue of some unknown prodigy, seemed to bury itself in the accessories of its triumph. For the throne opened up, descended, and the pedestal soon spread itself out over the mystery of the tomb.

Pierre thought he had been asleep when he could no longer perceive anything on the ground but a long white mound on to which the sun hung a few topazes and rubies on ridges of nascent frost. Half-crazed by fear, because he had just made contact with the Unknown, the ace of aces feverishly started up the engine of the apparatus. But his plane nearly capsized on take-off, so much was it shaken, jostled and swung by the elements that were fleeing in great cold whirlwinds, having accomplished their funerary task.

The aviator remembered then what Madame Wiscorney had often said to him:

"No levitation or apport is possible without the intervention of inferior beings. It is always dangerous to make them collaborate in spiritistic experiments. In order to dominate them, it requires souls more evolved than the common run of mortals possess."

....

....

....

When Pierre Montala landed on the improvised air-field organized at Courba, he was incapable of articulating a single word, and fever laid him out for three days.

In his delirium he repeated incessantly: "I've seen a soul! I've seen a soul float free!"

....

....

....

The Asia record was an occasion of unparalleled tri-umph for Pierre Montala, but he cut all the official recep-tions short in order to get back to Barbizon more rapidly. There, in Tussilia's former laboratory, the two spouses recounted to one another, one the final stage of the great Initiate's journey, and the other the kind grandmother's final lessons.

"Do you understand why those individuals whose science is evidently superior to ours don't simply and im-mediately reveal their secrets to the scientists of the pre-sent day?"

"Yes," said Maya. "It has already been observed that a great discovery, made before the mental level of human-kind has attained a certain degree, was either scorned or only employed for homicidal purposes. Great misfortunes have resulted from that. It's therefore necessary to wait for the fateful moment. All that is permitted to the Sages is to launch through space, once per cycle, a magnetic message giving the scientific explanation to a problem that is being sought. Evolved intelligences receive the message in the form of a sudden inspiration, and a discovery of genius is made. That laboratory discovery is then doggedly claimed by several scientists, in several countries, at the same time. They have, in fact, received the revelation simultaneously, via magnetic vibrations, and those mediums, without being aware of it, are making an individual glory out of something that was simply dictated to them."

"Do you really believe that our children will have the signal honor of…?"

"Why not? If the evolution of beings requires a new crossing, psychic or astral, it will always be necessary for a human larva to serve as the first link in the new chain. Our Gisèle will make an exceedingly lovely Madonna."

While conversing in that fashion, Pierre and Maya vaguely felt anguish and the malaise of doubt welling up within them. The great shadow of the old Hindu was not shoring up their faith, and their logic was poorly adapted to the modesty of their personalities. In order better to mediate and dream, they went on to the balcony where Tussilia had once had the vision of Kacyapa. Silence floated over Barbizon; the nocturnal breeze was scarcely perceptible and nothing could be heard in the forest but the sound of dead leaves sliding and skimming the ground. The sky was limpid and the stars were pricking tiny night-lights in the somber vault of the night.

Together, they raised their eyes.

"Do you believe that we'll ever reach one of those lamps?" said Pierre smiling.

"Why not?" said Maya, seriously.

"In fact, why not? Would our fathers have dreamed that India would only be a week's flight away today, and that the airplane isn't the Beast of the Apocalypse that will bring the promised God. It has feet, it has wings, fire emerges from its nostrils and runs through its veins. Maya, I'm afraid of not being great enough for my epoch!"

"What does it matter, since I love you anyway?

"Really, my love? Although amour is for us *as it is*, you'll give me credit for a little dreaming?"

"It seems to me that the sacred Science doesn't get in the way of our kisses..."

Once again, their evolved souls were confounded in the same ecstasy. And the age-old pleasure of the flesh redeemed—as it always does, a little—the crime once perpetrated by the Kastéhus of old on the first vanquished Awaïs.

Afterword
by the Translator

The published text of *[Amour]...tel qu'il est* is complete; it needs no addition, and there is a sense in which it cannot have any addition—but such as it is, it inevitably leads the reader to wonder about several unspecified issues, of which the most significant is perhaps the question of what the Redeemer is actually going to do to sort out the troubled situation of human life as described in the text.

We must work on the assumption, of course, that the text as published is the way its author intended it to be, even though we know full well that publishers sometimes employ copy-editors whose violations are sometimes as terrible, in their own context, as the depredations that the vile Kastéhus inflicted (and continue to inflict) on the poor Awaïs. In offering suggestions as to how the ideative schema of the text might be supplemented, however, I am not trying to guess what the author might have intended, let alone what she might have put into a fuller text before it was excised, but merely fantasizing.

The text does provide some information about the means of salvation that will deliver the descendants of humankind from the next cataclysm, which might or might not correspond to the metamorphic emergence of the King of the World, alias Brahytina or Brahymus, from the planetary cocoon. We know that the ovipares will ultimately triumph over the vivipares and that the sons of the Kastéhus will become sterile—in effect, that the male of the human species will cease to exist, and that it will become parthenogenetic as well as oviparous. We are also assured that the unparasitized females of the species will recover the wings that the Awaïs once had, or improved substitutes thereof, as a result of a definitive metamorphosis, in which the human nymph will finally complete its emergence from its present larval form. We know, too, that the flight of which the superhuman ovipares become capable, whether artificial, natural or some collaboration of the two, will take them away from the next earthly cataclysm into interplanetary space, perhaps all the way to the stars.

We have been told that the means of escape from the devastated Earth will involve submarines as well as aircraft, but it seems unlikely that the submarines in question will merely plunge beneath the agitated amniotic waves. With the aid of hindsight, it seems more likely that technology will bring about a fusion of the aircraft and the submarine to create something akin to the image of a spaceship that was beginning to take form in 1926, and that, in consequence, a significant part of Pierre's mission, and that of one or more of his children, will be to carry forward that technological sophistication of the mechanical power of extraterrestrial flight. The Redemption of humankind must, however, be a far more profound affair than a mere translocation to another planet, given that we know that the Redeemer will have to bring some kind of biological entity back from interplanetary space to provoke, and perhaps determine, a drastic biological metamorphosis.

Even though the Redeemer's primary mission is to deliver that extraterrestrial biological entity, it will probably be convenient, if not absolutely necessary for him or her be a biotechnologist of genius as well as an applied physicist—what would nowadays be called a genetic engineer—capable of assisting with the formation and maturation of the superhuman nymph that will be liberated from all the carnal evils resulting from the "original crime" of the Kastéhus. In so doing, he or she will, of course, merely be the instrument or midwife of a Destiny built into the schema of earthly evolution by the Astrological Entities governing its progress and its cycles alike—assuming, that is, that they are all working to the same plan, rather than conducting a weird war of their own in which the future is still to be settled; their ways are, alas, too mysterious for that to be readily discernible—but that does not means that the Redeemer will entitled to any less credit for the scientific genius that will allow that amazing task to be completed. He or she will obviously receive a little help from the telepathic messages broadcast by the Sages, but will surely have to take the final step or steps without such aid, because the knowledge of pre-cataclysmic pasts was obviously never adequate to secure Redemption.

Alas, the credit that will be due to the Redeemer does not make it any less likely that he or she might be crucified for his or her pains. The sons of the Kastéhus will undoubtedly run true to form, all the more so when threatened with extinction, and—wings or no wings—even Awaïs are no angels. Given the kind of supernatural help that the Redeemer seems to have in reserve, as well as the gift that will be transported back from the depths of interplanetary space, however, we can probably trust that he or she will triumph, and that the winged descendants of present-day humankind will set off for their new destiny elsewhere in the universe, equipped with new technologies, new bodies, and perhaps new souls as well, given that the present varieties of fluidic parasite seem to have plenty of defects of their own.

Having said all that, however, a few puzzles still remain, some minor and some major. One of the minor ones, albeit a niggling one, is the Crazy Rock? What is it, and what is it doing leaping about like that? Tussilia knew the secret, but never bothered to disclose it. All we really know from the text is that its activity increases when she or Maya are undertaking the exercises of Initiates. Given that we know that those involve levitation and "apportation" (what would now be called teleportation), however, the probability is that they are simply more-or-less random and essentially trivial shifts effected for practice.

The major puzzles, on the other hand, include the nature, agenda and destiny of the entity inside the world cocoon. There is no doubt that it is actively involved in the plot, but exactly what it is doing and why, and precisely what relationship it has with Tussilia, is profoundly unclear. We know that Tussilia was shackled by it before she became the Daughter of the Bungalow, but we do not know whether it released her voluntarily, or whether she was enabled to escape by some other entity or Force. It seems at times to want to disrupt the entire Redemption plan, by killing Pierre if it can, but it is difficult to detect the shadow of a motive for that. Is it really at war with some or all of the Astrological Entities, even though they seem to include its loving parents? Is it really at odds with the adherents of Brahma—who might be its "foster-brother," apparently—and if so, why? Tussilia refers to it as a prisoner and promises it liberation, but it is not obvious that it takes that view itself, and it is conceivable that it is not looking forward to its impending metamorphosis, any more than the sons of the Kastéhus are looking forward to theirs. If it sees its ultimate metamorphosis as a kind of extinction rather than a fulfillment, perhaps that is why it is fighting to delay the inevitable.

But what, in fact, is the King of the World going to metamorphose *into* when the final cataclysm comes? What will the imago of a world-grub look like, and what kind of life will it live? Will it be joining the population of Astrological Entities as an analogue of a butterfly-god, or will it just be another creature, analogous to a parasitic wasp, avid to parasitize some other poor creature elsewhere in the universe? Or will it be something else entirely—the possibilities are surely endless, even if we only take into account the insectile and religious analogies.

Then again, we also have to factor in the souls: the "nymphs of spirit," as they are described, somewhat enigmatically, at one point, and the third class of parasites making up portmanteau humankind—not to mention every other living thing, presumably including the King of the World, since it seems to have at least a rudimentary consciousness. Given that the Astrological Entities appear to be planners of a sort, perhaps they have them too, albeit of a different species from the various kinds that like to get their suckers into humankind. On the other hand, even if souls are the nymphs of spirit, and even if their existential aim is presently to return to the divine center like moths to a flame, that does not necessarily mean that they are finished with their own evolutionary process; perhaps is entirely possible that, beyond their seemingly-final metamorphosis, there is scope for further natural or supernatural selection, and that the universe still has potential for a much more elaborate and less flawed kind of intelligence, which really might be qualified, far more than anything we poor humans could ever produce, to call itself a Sage.

If that is the case—and who is really in a position to deny it?—perhaps the Plan of which the Astrological Entities and the King of the World are themselves mere instruments is really the work of Supersouls or Metasouls that have their own biology, evolution and progress, as well as their own weird life-cycle, and which can impose destinies even on the supposed makers of destiny, and maybe even, in the fullness of time, put one over on God—who would surely be a poor sort of creator if he could not or would not create a universe in which he might be superseded.

One would surely like to think so...at least, one would if one has the kind and sufficiency of imagination that enables one to get to grips with such truly adventurous texts as *[Amour]...tel qu'il est*.

SF & FANTASY

Adolphe Alhaiza. *Cybele*

Alphonse Allais. *The Adventures of Captain Cap*

Henri Allorge. *The Great Cataclysm*

Guy d'Armen. *Doc Ardan: The City of Gold and Lepers*

G.-J. Arnaud. *The Ice Company*

Charles Asselineau. *The Double Life*

Henri Austruy. *The Eupantophone; The Olotelepan; The Petitpaon Era*

Barillet-Lagargousse. *The Final War*

Cyprien Bérard. *The Vampire Lord Ruthwen*

S. Henry Berthoud. *Martyrs of Science*

Aloysius Bertrand. *Gaspard de la Nuit*

Richard Bessière. *The Gardens of the Apocalypse; The Masters of Silence*

Albert Bleunard. *Ever SMalher*

Félix Bodin. *The Novel of the Future*

Louis Boussenard. *Monsieur Synthesis*

Alphonse Brown. *City of Glass; The Conquest of the Air*

Emile Calvet. *In a Thousand Years*

André Caroff. *The Terror of Madame Atomos; Miss Atomos; The Return of Madame Atomos; The Mistake of Madame Atomos; The Monsters of Madame Atomos; The Revenge of Madame Atomos; The Resurrection of Madame Atomos; The Mark of Madame Atomos; The Spheres of Madame Atomos; The Wrath of Madame Atomos* (w/M. & Sylvie Stéphan)

Félicien Champsaur. *The Human Arrow; Ouha, King of the Apes; Pharaoh's Wife; Homo-Deus*

Didier de Chousy. *Ignis*

Jules Clarétie. *Obsession*

Michel Corday. *The Eternal Flame*

André Couvreur. *The Necessary Evil*; *Caresco, Superman; The Exploits of Professor Tornada* (3 vols.)

Captain Danrit. *Undersea Odyssey*

C. I. Defontenay. *Star (Psi Cassiopeia)*

Charles Derennes. *The People of the Pole*

Georges Dodds (anthologist). *The Missing Link*

Charles Dodeman. *The Silent Bomb*

Harry Dickson. *The Heir of Dracula; Harry Dickson vs. The Spider*

Jules Dornay. *Lord Ruthven Begins*
Alfred Driou. *The Adventures of a Parisian Aeronaut*
Sâr Dubnotal *vs. Jack the Ripper*
Alexandre Dumas. *The Return of Lord Ruthven*
Renée Dunan. *Baal*
J.-C. Dunyach. *The Night Orchid; The Thieves of Silence*
Henri Duvernois. *The Man Who Found Himself*
Achille Eyraud. *Voyage to Venus*
Henri Falk. *The Age of Lead*
Paul Féval. *Anne of the Isles; Knightshade; Revenants; Vampire City; The Vampire Countess; The Wandering Jew's Daughter*
Paul Féval, *fils. Felifax, the Tiger-Man*
Charles de Fieux. *Lamékis*
Louis Forest. *Someone is Stealing Children in Paris*
Arnould Galopin. *Doctor Omega*; *Doctor Omega and the Shadowmen* (anthology)
Judith Gautier. *Isoline and the Serpent-Flower*
H. Gayar. *The Marvelous Adventures of Serge Myrandhal on Mars*
G.L. Gick. *Harry Dickson and the Werewolf of Rutherford Grange*
Delphine de Girardin. *Balzac's Cane*
Léon Gozlan. *The Vampire of the Val-de-Grâce*
Edmond Haraucourt. *Illusions of Immortality; Daah, the First Human*
Nathalie Henneberg. *The Green Gods*
Eugène Hennebert. *The Enchanted City*
V. Hugo, P. Foucher & P. Meurice. *The Hunchback of Notre-Dame*
Romain d'Huissier. *Hexagon: Dark Matter*
Jules Janin. *The Magnetized Corpse*
Michel Jeury. *Chronolysis*
Gustave Kahn. *The Tale of Gold and Silence*
Gérard Klein. *The Mote in Time's Eye*
Fernand Kolney. *Love in 5000 Years*
Paul Lacroix. *Danse Macabre*
Louis-Guillaume de La Follie. *The Unpretentious Philosopher*
Jean de La Hire. *Enter the Nyctalope; The Nyctalope on Mars; The Nyctalope vs. Lucifer; The Nyctalope Steps In; Night of the Nyctalope; Return of the Nyctalope; The Fiery Wheel*
Etienne-Léon de Lamothe-Langon. *The Virgin Vampire*
André Laurie. *Spiridon*
Gabriel de Lautrec. *The Vengeance of the Oval Portrait*
Alain le Drimeur. *The Future City*

Georges Le Faure & Henri de Graffigny. *The Extraordinary Adventures of a Russian Scientist Across the Solar System* (2 vols.)
Gustave Le Rouge. *The Mysterious Doctor Cornelius* (3 vols.); *The Vampires of Mars; The Dominion of the World* (w/Gustave Guitton) (4 vols.)
Jules Lermina. *Mysteryville; Panic in Paris; To-Ho and the Gold Destroyers; The Secret of Zippeliu; The Battle of Strasbourg*
André Lichtenberger. *The Centaurs; The Children of the Crab*
Listonai. *The Philosophical Voyager*
Jean-Marc & Randy Lofficier. *Edgar Allan Poe on Mars; The Katrina Protocol; Pacifica; Robonocchio; Return of the Nyctalope;* (anthologists) *Tales of the Shadowmen 1-11; The Vampire Almanac*
Xavier Mauméjean. *The League of Heroes*
Joseph Méry. *The Tower of Destiny*
Hippolyte Mettais. *The Year 5865; Paris Before the Deluge*
Louise Michel. *The Human Microbes; The New World*
Tony Moilin. *Paris in the Year 2000*
José Moselli. *Illa's End*
John-Antoine Nau. *Enemy Force*
Marie Nizet. *Captain Vampire*
C. Nodier, A. Beraud & Toussaint-Merle. *Frankenstein*
Henri de Parville. *An Inhabitant of the Planet Mars*
Gaston de Pawlowski. *Journey to the Land of the 4th Dimension*
Georges Pellerin. *The World in 2000 Years*
Ernest Pérochon. *The Frenetic People*
Pierre Pelot. *The Child Who Walked on the Sky*
J. Polidori, C. Nodier, E. Scribe. *Lord Ruthven the Vampire*
P.-A. Ponson du Terrail. *The Vampire and the Devil's Son; The Immortal Woman*
Georges Price. *The Missing Men of the Sirius*
Edgar Quinet. *Ahasuerus; The Enchanter Merlin*
Henri de Régnier. *A Surfeit of Mirrors*
Maurice Renard. *The Blue Peril; Doctor Lerne; The Doctored Man; A Man Among the Microbes; The Master of Light*
Jean Richepin. *The Wing; The Crazy Corner*
Albert Robida. *The Adventures of Saturnin Farandoul; The Clock of the Centuries; Chalet in the Sky; The Electric Life*
J.-H. Rosny Aîné. *Helgvor of the Blue River; The Givreuse Enigma; The Mysterious Force; The Navigators of Space; Vamireh; The World of the Variants; The Young Vampire*
Marcel Rouff. *Journey to the Inverted World*

Léonie Rouzade. *The World Turned Upside Down*

Han Ryner. *The Superhumans; The Human Ant*

Pierre de Selenes: *An Unknown World*

Angelo de Sorr. *The Vampires of London*

Brian Stableford. *The New Faust at the Tragicomique;The Empire of the Necromancers (The Shadow of Frankenstein; Frankenstein and the Vampire Countess; Frankenstein in London); Sherlock Holmes & The Vampires of Eternity; The Stones of Camelot; The Wayward Muse.* (anthologist) *News from the Moon; The Germans on Venus; The Supreme Progress; The World Above the World; Nemoville; Investigations of the Future; The Conqueror of Death; The Revolt of the Machines; The Man With the Blue Face*

Jacques Spitz. *The Eye of Purgatory*

Kurt Steiner. *Ortog*

Eugène Thébault. *Radio-Terror*

C.-F. Tiphaigne de La Roche. *Amilec*

Simon Tyssot de Patot. *The Strange Voyages of Jacques Massé and Pierre de Mésange*

Louis Ulbach. *Prince Bonifacio*

Théo Varlet. *The Golden Rock. The Xenobiotic Invasion; The Castaways of Eros; Timeslip Troopers* (w/André Blandin); *The Martian Epic* (w/Octave Joncquel)

Pierre Véron. *The Merchants of Health*

Paul Vibert. *The Mysterious Fluid*

Villiers de l'Isle-Adam. *The Scaffold; The Vampire Soul*

Philippe Ward. *Artahe ; The Song of Montségur* (w/Sylvie Miller) *Manhattan Ghost* (w/Mickael Laguerre)

MYSTERIES & THRILLERS

M. Allain & P. Souvestre. *The Daughter of Fantômas*

A. Anicet-Bourgeois, Lucien Dabril. *Rocambole*

A. Bernède. *Belphegor*; *Judex* (w/Louis Feuillade); *The Return of Judex* (w/Louis Feuillade); *The Shadow of Judex*

A. Bisson & G. Livet. *Nick Carter vs. Fantômas*

V. Darlay & H. de Gorsse. *Arsène Lupin vs. Sherlock Holmes: The Stage Play*

Séamas Duffy. *Sherlock Holmes in Paris*

Paul Féval. *Gentlemen of the Night; John Devil; The Black Coats ('Salem Street; The Invisible Weapon; The Parisian Jungle; The*

Companions of the Treasure; Heart of Steel; The Cadet Gang; The Sword-Swallower)

Emile Gaboriau. *Monsieur Lecoq*

Goron & Emile Gautier. *Spawn of the Penitentiary*

Paul d'Ivoi. *Around the World on Five Sous* (w/Henri Chabrillat)

Rick Lai. *Shadows of the Opera: Retribution in Blood; Sisters of the Shadows: The Curse of Cagliostro*

Steve Leadley. *Sherlock Holmes: The Circle of Blood*

Maurice Leblanc. *Arsène Lupin vs. Countess Cagliostro; Arsène Lupin vs. Sherlock Holmes (The Blonde Phantom; The Hollow Needle); The Many Faces of Arsène Lupin; The Island of the Thirty Coffins*

Gaston Leroux. *Chéri-Bibi; The Phantom of the Opera; Rouletabille & the Mystery of the Yellow Room; Rouletabille at Krupp's*

Richard Marsh. *The Complete Adventures of Judith Lee*

William Patrick Maynard. *The Terror of Fu Manchu; The Destiny of Fu Manchu*

Frank J. Morlock. *Sherlock Holmes: The Grand Horizontals; Sherlock Holmes vs Jack the Ripper*

Jean Petithuguenin. *The Adventures of Ethel King*

Antonin Reschal. *The Adventures of Miss Boston*

P. de Wattyne & Y. Walter. *Sherlock Holmes vs. Fantômas*

David White. *Fantômas in America*

Pierre Yrondy. *The Adventures of Thérèse Arnaud*

Victor Margueritte. *The Bacheloress; The Companion; The Couple*

SCREENPLAYS

Mike Baron. *The Iron Triangle*

Emma Bull & Will Shetterly. *Nightspeeder; War for the Oaks*

Gerry Conway & Roy Thomas. *Doc Dynamo*

Steve Englehart. *Majorca*

James Hudnall. *The Devastator*

Jean-Marc & Randy Lofficier. *Royal Flush*

J.-M. & R. Lofficier & Marc Agapit. *Despair*

J.-M. & R. Lofficier & Joël Houssin. *City*

Andrew Paquette. *Peripheral Vision*

Robert L. Robinson, Jr. *Judex*

R. Thomas, J. Hendler & L. Sprague de Camp. *Rivers of Time*